THE MAIDEN VOYAGE OF THE MARYANN

Linda A. Reed

KEYES CANYON PRESS

SAN MIGUEL, CALIFORNIA

ISBN 978-0-9850074-1-6 (Print)

ISBN 978-0-9850074-0-9 (eBook)

Publisher's Note: This is a work of fiction. Names, characters, places, and incidents are a product of the author's imagination. Locales and public names are sometimes used for atmospheric purposes. Any resemblance to actual people, living or dead, or to businesses, companies, events, institutions, or locales is completely coincidental.

Keyes Canyon Press

San Miguel, CA 93451

www.keyescanyonpress.com

The Maiden Voyage of The Maryann/ Linda A. Reed. -- 1st ed.

DEDICATED TO my husband Ken Reed and my mother Pat Gross, whose never-ending encouragement, ideas, and edits nudged me forward and kept me going.

SPECIAL THANKS TO The Cambria Writer's Workshop and Writer' Digest – whose competitions and judges feedback helped improve this manuscript immeasurably.

A good traveler has no fixed plans and is not intent on arriving.

—LAO TZU

LINEAGE OF CHARACTERS (year born)

Mary (1702)

Ann (1719)

Ester (1739)

Elizabeth (1765)

Isabel (1785)

Elaine (1805)

Sarah (1830)

Sophia (1855)

Winifred (Winnie) (1875)

Madeline (Maddie) (1890)

Caroline (1915)

Isadora (Izzie) (1935)

Margaret (Maggie) (1960)

Emily (1980)

LOOMINGS

The rider tore along the wooded path, fear charging his heart to beat furiously. He knew his long ride and perhaps his short life neared an end. At last through the trees he could see the dark ship anchored silently offshore, swaying slowly with the currents of the sheltered bay, and rounding the bend he saw the silhouette of a man, ghostly gray in the light of the full moon. He slowed his pace as he approached the water's edge. A dangerous man, a pirate feared by all who sailed the seas or lived near its shores, waited for him.

He dismounted and walked tentatively towards the pirate. He'd traveled all night, turning the message over and over in his mind, examining every angle, trying to find a way to deliver the missive without it sounding as bad as he knew it to be. He doubted the pirate wanted to know all the reasons for the message, the politics, and personal fortunes that were wrapped up in the decision to stop him. Calm prudence seemed the best course.

The pirate towered well over six feet, a menacing presence in daylight and even more so at night. A large tri-corner hat with a flamboyant white feather made his height appear even greater. In the blush of morning sun, the rider saw the pirate wore a dark red jacket and a clean, ruffled white shirt, in stark contrast to his long ragged black beard and mustache. The gleam of a steel cutlass glinted at his side, secured by a golden cord around his waist. He couldn't see all this in the shadows of the trees, but the rider knew it to be so, as others had told it to him in preparation for his mission. The pirate looked every bit that of a proper gentleman who had just stepped out of a tavern on his way to his well-kept home and his fashionable wife. Nothing could be further from the truth.

"What have ye?" His voice was deep and gruff. Though it had weariness to it as if the tall man knew what the message would be yet needed to hear it aloud for it to be true.

The rider took a deep breath. Despite the length of time he had dwelt on how the message would sound, nothing could guarantee he would live through its telling. Cautiously he began,

"Governor Spotswood is sending a ship, captained by a Lieutenant Maynard. They have orders to kill you."

He left it at that. The less said the less chance of being shot where he stood or run through by the cutlass.

The pirate grunted, kicked the ground with a black boot adorned with a large silver buckle, and then spat on the ground. The rider didn't move a muscle until with a wave of his hand the pirate dismissed him. He melted back into the dark of the woods, grateful to have survived an encounter with Blackbeard, the notorious pirate.

CHAPTER ONE

EMILY

Emily's fingers clung to the top of the mast, cold and damp in the fog. Despite the calm air of the grey cloud that surrounded her; the wooden pole she wrapped her arms around swayed from side to side and fear gripped every muscle in her body. How exactly had she gotten here? She remembered climbing up; compelled by something she couldn't understand. The moon had been out only moments before she put her foot on the first square of the rigging, yet as she put one hand over the other to climb, the cold damp air grew thicker until she could see only the mast.

Below the wooden mast, splintered and weathered, lay the battered deck of a pirate ship. Below, in the ship's galley, huddled thirteen women who, if Emily understood it all correctly, were her ancestors. One said she was her biological mother. Emily had learned of her own adoption only weeks ago, a revelation made by her mother as Emily filled out a medical form. The topic of family diseases came up and Sydney, the woman she thought of as her mother, broke down in tears and revealed a secret she'd kept Emily's whole life. Emily ran out of the room, confused, and scared.

Is that how she arrived on top of a ship's mast? Could the shock have driven her out of her mind? Emily remembered feeling so out of sorts, unsure who she really was now, that she talked a friend into going to a bar in Charleston, far from home and everyone who knew her. There she had met Mark, good-looking and likable, who played the drums for the band. He had the type of free spirit she imagined her real family had. It didn't take much for them to get into bed together, her first time, though she didn't let on. Did the sin of that act drive her here?

Don't be silly, she told herself. You're up here because it is your turn, and the ship could ram into the rocks. The fog made any attempt to see outcroppings impossible, so she hung on and prayed for clear skies.

Her mind wandered to the first time she saw the deck of *The Maryann*. It had been days before, a week maybe, hard to tell with no electricity or clocks. Her phone had died but proved useless anyway without cell coverage. It might have even stopped working the minute she walked into the tea shop on East Bay Street.

The shop looked like someone had pulled it off a back shelf, fluffed it out, and plunked it on the sidewalk between two trendy boutiques. The paint - white at some point – was now a combination of bare wood and faded tint. Its façade matched the sky, grey, blotchy, and dismal. The other shops along the bustling street radiated energy of the now. This shop seemed oblivious to time or calendar and determined to keep its own course.

Emily felt sympathy for the little shop. It felt out of place, and she could relate to that. At that moment Emily felt very out of place. The last few weeks had been a deviation from her normal, ordered existence. She thrived on the drumbeat of eat, sleep, work. Yet, in the span of a few weeks, she had learned she had been adopted and then, almost immediately that she had foolishly gotten herself pregnant.

The bell attached to the top of the door frame rang as she crossed the threshold and stepped into the shop. Like an attic, things crowded the floor and shelves, old ship bells, chronographs, and life-saving rings. Emily stood in the center of the shop and allowed her eyes to scan the room in an unfocused way. The items had a familiar feel despite her lack of sailing experience. She often dreamed of oceans and sailing ships but had never actually spent much time in or on the water.

Her mother, Sydney, an elegant lithe woman, had been a dancer before she retired to raise Emily. She filled Emily's weekends with ballet recitals, opera, classical concerts with the philharmonic, and endless visits to the Metropolitan Art Museum. She could identify ballets by the orchestra's first notes, and painters by their brush strokes. Yet, her awareness of their talent didn't elicit any of it in her. Attempts to draw, dance, or play music, came out stilted and plodding, with no evidence of passion

7

in any of it. Her mother tried not to show her disappointment, but the words slipped out occasionally and Emily could hear it in her voice.

"Keep trying dear, art is in your blood, I just know it, and what's in your blood will always come out in time."

She couldn't say it, but Emily knew the arts didn't flow in her blood, especially now that she knew that someone else's blood flowed through her veins. Some strange couple she didn't know, and had no hope to know, gave her the unique dimple on her cheek and red-hued hair. Emily had been angry at first. Over the last few weeks, as she learned the story of her adoption, she became more accepting and even excited to wonder what really did run in her blood.

She imagined her real parents, wealthy and now lonely, ready to welcome her back into their lives. Sydney shaped Emily's childhood around the activities Sydney loved, activities Emily sat through. A wave of nausea swept over her, which reminded her of the baby, she had gotten herself knocked up. What talents would flow from her to her baby?

'Her baby' just didn't sound right, and even thinking about it made her heart skip a beat.

Towards the back of the shop and she saw a woman, sitting on a stool behind a makeshift counter. An old brass cash register occupied half the counter space and Emily wondered whether it functioned.

Freckles dusted the woman's nose and a bandanna held back her long, strawberry-blond hair.

"You look like you could use a cup of nice hot tea."

Emily gaped at the woman as her voice penetrated Emily's silent contemplations, a voice like hot cocoa poured steaming, thick and sweet into a cup.

"Tea would be nice." Emily agreed.

The shop woman waved her to a doorway in the back, covered with a darkly patterned fabric, pulled back and held in place with a large fish hook. Gold fringe dangled from the edges of the fabric. The woman herself wore an explosion of bright colors on a loose top and skirt.

The light dimmed in the back, but as Emily's eyes adjusted, she could see two tables covered with colorful tablecloths and an eclectic mix of chairs. She chose a table and sat down. She watched the woman move about and thought that she looked just like a gypsy, or at least the ones she'd seen in movies.

The woman went to a counter in the back, made from a wood plank set on two large wooden barrels, and poured hot water from a standard aluminum percolator coffee pot into a delicate English teapot decorated with pink roses. Huge blue hoop earrings shimmered as she reached into an earthenware jar and pulled out a handful of tea leaves.

Emily could smell the tea as it went into the teapot. Then the woman closed her eyes, began to swirl the pot, and chant in a low incantation. Moments later she brought the teapot and the only two matching teacups over to the table. With great care, she set the cups down, turned the handles to face away from Emily, and poured out the tea. The golden-brown liquid flowed from the teapot.

"When you're finished, I will read the leaves for you." She had a thick warm accent, "I'm sure it will be very interesting for you." Her eyes held Emily's for a moment and then she too sat down and carefully picked up her cup and sipped the hot tea.

They drank in silence. The tea tasted stronger than her typical cup of English Breakfast Tea and had a slight bite to it. Emily would have left it were it not for the watchful shopkeeper, who hovered, waiting to read the leaves. She drank as much as she could and set the cup back down. Dark bits of leaves swirled at the bottom. The woman quickly swooped in and began to read the leaves.

Her blue earrings dangled down and tapped the sides of the cups as she hunched intently over Emily's cup and mumbled to herself. Emily wondered if this woman meant her harm. She had never read of a kidnapping that started out this way, not that she had read all that many stories about kidnaps. After what seemed like an eternity the women looked up.

"You are worried about the baby."

Emily held her breath. How had this woman, a woman she had just met, known about the baby? She had told no one about the pregnancy, not even her mother. She had only learned herself and couldn't show it yet.

Perhaps the shame showed on her face. The hours of anxiety she had lived since the blue indicator on the pregnancy test, she had bought at the drug store and peed on it at home. The blue patch on the stick signaled the worst possible outcome Emily could have imagined. Her limbs had felt heavy like she sank in molasses while all the things she hoped to accomplish paraded by. She felt overtaken by a mistake. Her thoughts swirled, should I end the pregnancy or have the child and raise it, or have the child and give it away in adoption, like me. Given away sounded so heartless. The irony of the situation was not lost on her.

What kind of a mother would she make if her first thoughts were how do I get out of this, she wondered. What kind of mother am I to get pregnant this way? I'm an idiot, that's what kind.

Emily felt a powerful sense of responsibility in every aspect of her life. Before she made any decisions about this baby, she felt an obligation to tell the father. She had met Mark about a month ago at Dooley's, a popular bar in town. He seemed nice enough and different from the guys at work. A musician. The kind who worked at a funeral home and she never expected to see again. They had hooked up the day after Emily learned of her adoption. It had been wild and out-of-character conduct and regret overwhelmed her. She didn't ever want to see him and relive the embarrassment of that night. She thought she could put it behind her as a growth experience that would grow dim with time. Oh, if only that were the case.

"How do you know?" Emily asked.

"Bedalia knows much others do not." The shopkeeper continued to study the cup.

"Yeah well, I'd rather others not know. This isn't my proudest moment."

"How did the father take the news?" Bedalia asked though it seemed clear to Emily that the woman already knew the answer.

"He took it well, I guess. Seems like he'll do the right thing, whatever that turns out to be."

"The right thing is the right thing."

"I'm not sure what that means. Is it the right thing to end the pregnancy or to have the baby and give it away? The idea of raising a baby right now is terrifying, I'm not ready to be a mother, I'm scared, and I don't have the first idea what to do."

"The right thing is only right for you. No one can or should tell you what is right for you."

"That's not very helpful."

"You are strong; whatever you chose, you will do well."

Bedalia's self-help aphorisms didn't sit well with Emily. Anger and denial competed like dogs fighting for a bone.

"That's where you're wrong. I'm not strong, I'm a coward. I'm a follower and I like to fit in with the crowd. Lately, I've just felt like throwing up a lot."

Why she felt she needed to explain that to this strange woman Emily couldn't fathom. The words formed as she spoke;

she had not contemplated her strengths or weaknesses like this before.

The woman swirled the teacup again, eyes now closed, and a smile grew on her face.

"I know your mother."

Emily's eyebrows shot up, "Are you saying you know my biological mother or my adopted mother?"

"Your true mother. I've been waiting for you to visit my little shop. I have something for you from her," and with that Bedalia rose and left the room.

Emily couldn't move. This woman is spooky. I should get out of this place as fast as I can.

She tried but couldn't move any of her leg muscles. Frozen to the chair, not through anything Bedalia had done, Emily felt sure of that, but more her body didn't want to cooperate with her brain's message to flee. This strange woman she had just met seemed to know her better than she knew herself. How could that be? She had never been in this shop, had never seen the woman, yet she knew about the baby and her own adoption. This stranger knew two of the biggest secrets Emily had in her life. Even her own mother didn't know about the pregnancy. The disappointment of her perfect daughter having done something so irresponsible would destroy their relationship. How could this woman know?

After a short delay, Bedalia returned with a leather pouch. It had a drawstring at the top, pulled tight by a pink silk cord. She laid it carefully on the table in front of Emily. The pouch looked mostly empty although the bottom had a slight bulge. Emily picked it up and slowly undid the knot in the pink silk cord then tilted the pouch and a small gold heart-shaped locket slid out onto the table.

The locket had filigree etched on the cover which mirrored the heart shape. Emily picked it up and turned it over in her hand. It felt warm in her palm like the love of the heart radiated out. She carefully pushed the little latch on the side and opened the locket to reveal a black and white photograph of a woman, a woman with dark hair and light eyes, just like Emily's auburn hair and green eyes.

Not a picture of the woman who had raised her, the woman who gave up a dancer's career to give her a home and love. Rather, the picture of the woman who had borne her and delivered her into the arms of another family. Emily held a picture of her biological mother. She could barely breathe.

"What is her name?" she asked.

"Margaret, but everyone calls her Maggie."

Emily repeated the name, Maggie, Maggie, Margaret, Maggie.

"What is her last name?"

"Her last name is not important."

"Her last name is especially important to me; it's how I'll find her. I want to meet her, see what she's like, and understand why she gave me up!"

The face in the picture looked kind, not the face of a crazed woman incapable of raising a child. Emily closed the locket and then quickly reopened it. The woman's smile still greeted her.

"You will not need her last name to find her. She waits for you."

"Waits? Waits where? How does she know where I am?"

"So many questions, I can tell you like order. Life doesn't go ordered or planned. We think it does, but it doesn't. Let life happen and you will find your mother."

Emily felt anger and frustration bubble up inside and tighten in her throat. The women knew so much about her yet would not give her mother's last name. How did Bedalia know that Emily liked things planned out, orderly and structured? Her career choice as an engineer had reflected that preference. Nothing wrong with that. True, she swam in uncharted waters with an accidental pregnancy, the stress of learning her mother wasn't really her mother and now news that her biological mother waited for her. Emily preferred to plan, not just let life happen. She set the goal, planned the approach, and went after it. That's exactly how I'll deal with all this she told herself

Emily moved her toes without thought. She found she could now squirm in her seat and that her legs moved again. She stood up fast and her head spun a bit. She held onto the chair back until her head cleared.

"I'm leaving now," she called out.

"As you wish."

Politeness forced Emily to thank Bedalia for the tea and the locket to which the woman nodded. Grateful the tea had settled Emily's stomach; she placed the locket around her neck and walked out of the back room. The white light of an overcast sky filtered through the dust on the windows and filled the room with an enchanting glow, strangely bright after the dark of the back room.

She fingered the locket with her right hand as she walked through the tea shop and opened the front door. She had been anxious to get out of the shop, yet now that she could leave, she felt reluctant to sever the tie with someone who knew her mother. I'll find my mother myself, she thought, I don't need her help.

Emily stepped out of the tea shop and stopped abruptly. The street had vanished. The trendy boutiques and t-shirt shops had disappeared. The sun shone bright, and she stood on the deck of a large wooden ship that rocked back and forth on the calm waters of a sheltered cove.

She looked behind her back into the tea shop, still filled with a jumble of nautical relics. The door to the back room had vanished though and the whole room looked more like a storage room than a tea shop.

Emily turned around and saw she stood on the deck of a ship, an old ship. Many sets of eyes - too many to count - watched her. Behind her, Bedalia walked through the shop door. The others, all women, seemed to know her and accept that she had affected some type of magic on Emily. She fought the urge to

16

faint; too much had happened too fast. Surely this must be a dream, or she had been drugged. I'll wake up from this and it will all be gone. Maybe the baby is a bad dream too. As dreams go, she had to concede, this one felt realistic. Bedalia smiled at Emily as she passed on her way to a bell that hung by a thick rope from the wheel deck railing.

"Emily is the last of you... soon we will return to where we started."

The women listened to Bedalia's words as if made sense. To Emily, they contained no meaning, no hints of rational thought. Return to where exactly? She scanned the women who stood on the ship's deck and one face jumped out at her. As impossible as it seemed, the face she had just seen in the locket - the same locket that now hung from her neck – stood in front of her. Her hand went to the gold fob where it lay on her chest, the locket that held the face of the woman who had born her into this world and given her away. A face she had held out only the barest of hope to ever see.

Maggie stepped forward out of the crowd of women to approach Emily.

It is impossible that this is my biological mother?

"Emily? Is that you?" She saw the woman from the locket - even more beautiful than the little black and white picture. Her hair fell thick and auburn, her eyes were green, and her nose turned up at the end the exact same way Emily's did.

17

Emily couldn't speak, so she nodded. She didn't know whether to be happy or sad, excited, or scared, angry, or relieved. How could her birth mother be standing there? Is this what Bedalia had meant when she said Maggie waited for Emily?

"I didn't know if they would keep the name I gave you."

Emily couldn't speak, she nodded her head yes, tears stung her eyes, and her vision blurred.

"You're beautiful," Maggie said.

"It seems I have you to thank for that."

"I suppose there is some truth to that." Maggie's voice cracked. She took her daughter into her arms and hugged her as if to make up for the lost time. After a time, short or long Emily didn't know, she pulled away from the embrace.

"I despaired to give you up, but I knew the life you would have with the people that adopted you would be much better than the one you'd have with me."

Emily had craved to hear these words. Why she had been given up for adoption. Now that she had heard them, she didn't feel the sense of relief she expected. Instead, she felt disappointed. Maggie's reasons sounded like the ones she had thought of to figure out what to do with the baby she carried.

"I'd like to know more about your life and your decision," she told Maggie, "seems I need to make a similar one."

"Are you pregnant?" Maggie asked and Emily dropped her head in shame. While their similar situations had some measure of symmetry, she still felt deep embarrassment that her first contact with her biological mother should be marred by her own unplanned pregnancy. She felt a twinge in her stomach as a bit of nausea she had felt for the last week returned, amplified by the movement of the ship. She looked again at the ship with its dull wood rails and tattered sails.

"Where am I?" Emily asked.

"You are aboard *The Maryann*, a decrepit ship that just traveled through time to pick us all up, and is now headed back to its own time, which I think is around 1719 or so. We've all just arrived as you did. Sounds crazy, doesn't it?"

Emily didn't think Maggie made any more sense than Bedalia.

"That's the craziest thing I've ever heard. There must have been something in that tea I had in that shop which," Emily gestured back to the doorway, which now looked nothing like the door to the tea shop, "appears to have vanished."

"The tea shop is a portal to this ship. I've just learned this all myself, so I don't know how it works, but it's how we all got here. All except Mary and Bedalia that is."

"Who are Mary and Bedalia?"

"Well, Mary is easier to explain than Bedalia. Mary is your many times great-grandmother. I don't know how many greats there are between you and her, but it is a lot. She is the original mother of us all. All these women are your family, except Bedalia. She is the woman you met in the tea shop, as we all did. She isn't related to any of us, and aside from being a ghost or something

19

like that, I'm not sure how she is connected to or why she helps Mary."

Maggie's eyes sparked a bit at the suggestion of a mystery, and she had a mischievous smile.

"A ghost? Seriously?"

"Don't you believe in ghosts?"

"Well, not really, I guess, I haven't spent much time thinking about it. I suppose they could exist; I haven't seen any studies on it or anything."

Emily liked to have data to support her beliefs. She could imagine the reaction of her engineering friends at Williams Engineering if she told them she believed in ghosts. They would laugh at her for days.

"We'll have plenty of time to talk later. For now, let's go meet the others." Maggie linked arms with Emily and led her over to the larger group.

"Ladies, I would like to introduce you to Emily, my daughter." Applause erupted and one by one the ladies raised their hands and introduced themselves.

"I'm Isadora, Maggie's mother, and your grandmother. Welcome. You can call me Izzie."

"I'm Caroline, Izzie's mother, and your great grandmother," and around they went. Emily's head spun with all the names and greats that preceded the word mother. Counting Emily and Mary there were fourteen women in total: Ann, Ester, Elizabeth, Isabel, Elaine, Sarah, Sophia, Winnie, Madeline,

Caroline, Isadora, and Maggie. No one mentioned their last name, the men in their lives played just a bit part in each of their stories and their names were inconsequential.

Bedalia avoided the introductions altogether. She watched from an out-of-the-way spot over by the bell. As the sound of introductions wound down, she stepped closer to the bell and grabbed the rope connected to the clapper in the center of the bell. The sound waves reverberated like a wave of energy across the deck and Emily felt faint. The sunny sky faded to black, and Emily felt all the air in her lungs whoosh out, then with a snap the pressure released, and she gulped in the fresh air.

The bright sun cut through the black and her head began to clear. The bell had stopped, and Emily could tell all her relatives had experienced the same strange sensations. They appeared to have expected it though and held onto each other and the ship's rail. Bedalia alone seemed unaffected. She looked over the group of women, and when they had all recovered announced, and when they had all recovered announced, "We are back. Now find your treasure."

CHAPTER TWO

EMILY

The second night Isabel stuck her head out the port and said, "Can't see a thing out there, fog has moved in. I think we're safe, but not really knowing these waters, we could drift into rocks. Any suggestions on what to do?"

She had inherited Blackbeard's fierce eyes, which were mahogany brown and ringed in black, making them appear as black as coal. Her thick hair was deep brown, which she wore pulled back to keep it from flying around in the wind.

"I just went up there, Isabel, it was clear and calm. What happened?" Emily had spent the last two days repairing sails and polishing every inch of the ship, she didn't want anything to happen to a boat that had begun to feel like a person.

"I don't know, one minute the sails are luffing the next dead calm. Spooky."

"We need to stow the sails. We could drift into something," said Madeline. Since she had been quiet up till now, everyone took note. All eyes turned to Henry who nodded in agreement.

"One of you'll have to go, I have a bad leg," he added, patting his right leg.

Stowing the sail meant someone had to climb up the tall tree trunk of a pole in the dark and fog. There was silence as the women thought about the task at hand, each hoping someone else would step forward. All eyes were on the wooden table as if eye contact would signal a willingness to go aloft into the rigging, which would be slippery, cold, and dangerous. Isabel stood waiting. "I'm afraid of heights. Someone else will have to do it."

Emily felt the pull of responsibility and she knew it was only a matter of time before she would stand up and volunteer. Climbing the ropes and tying off the sails during broad daylight was hard enough. A wrong step and she would fall, likely to her death. She hated this about herself. She couldn't say no to requests for volunteers for anything. Emily took a deep breath and stood up.

"I'll go."

As she stood there was an audible sigh of relief. No one jumped in to do it for her. Fine, she thought.

"All right then, back in a few," she said with more cheer than she felt and turned to climb the stairs to the deck.

As she climbed the stairs it grew quieter and quieter with every step of the stairs. When she stepped onto the deck and looked back the pool of light around the table of women was gone, inky darkness swallowing her.

This is weird, she thought as she stepped outside and the textured darkness of the cold, musty fog assaulted all her senses at once. The dampness enveloped her in its clammy grayness. Sea salt and dank seaweed smell flooded her nostrils and she gasped as the air hit her nose, her head swimming. The air was so close she felt wrapped in a damp cold towel.

Emily stood still, trying to adapt. Isabel had been right about the visibility — she held up her hand to her face, almost touching her nose, and could barely see it.

This isn't the usual fog we get along the coast, she thought, I don't like it.

Tentatively she inched forward, knowing that the main mast roping was ahead and to either side. She decided to climb the ropes instead of the mast and veered right. It seemed to take forever to negotiate the fifteen feet from the door to the ropes. Emily almost swam the distance, her feet inching along and her arms slowly waving in front of her to avoid hitting anything unexpected. Her heart pounded in her chest with fear.

Yes, this is a nightmare, dark, cold, and scary. She thought about the things she expected to see or feel on deck: ropes, buckets, mops, deck, and the solid wooden mast. She whooped a little 'wahoo' when her hands felt the solid heft of the railing and the ropes and looking up into the dark gray emptiness found a first step and handhold and she slowly began to climb.

25

Each step up was a small victory yet with each step her heart and head felt heavier and heavier. What was she doing here anyway, what message was this dream trying to send her?

Up she climbed, carefully placing her feet on ropes when they presented themselves. The stillness of the fog was slowly giving way to a low murmur, like the sound of hundreds of people all talking at once at the other end of a large hall. She couldn't see the source of the sound and decided it was in her head.

She couldn't tell how far she had gone; the darkness was distorting her perception. Up she climbed, hands tentatively grabbing damp, slick ropes and her feet working to find purchase. Up she climbed and the murmur built, words slowly emerging, 'unwanted,' 'bad mother,' 'irresponsible.' Pictures flooded her mind unbidden with every word. All these women had been unwanted yet now they were wanted by each other.

"I don't know what to do," she called out to the voices.

By the time she reached the mizzen mast, she was gasping for breath and arguing angrily with the voices.

"This wasn't my choice!" she shouted, and she almost bumped into Bedalia.

"What the...what are you doing here?" Emily asked. "Where are those voices coming from?"

Bedalia was standing on the mizzen mast as if standing on flat land.

"I don't hear voices," Bedalia calmly replied, "you hear voices?"

26

"Yes, I hear voices," she replied curtly, then blurted "who are you and why am I here?"

"I was going to ask you. Why do you think you're here?" Her bright blouse was visible in the fog as if some unreal light shone from within.

"I don't know, one minute I'm in your tea shop and the next I'm on a ship in some weird time warp."

"Do you want to go back? I can make that happen in the blink of an eye." She smiled. Her eyes were dark, endlessly dark, windows to a soul Emily couldn't get a fix on.

"Go back to what, before I got pregnant? Can you undo that mistake?"

The pregnancy, that's what this is all about Emily realized, my mind is trying to work through whether to keep the baby or not.

Somehow, in a dream state, Emily was sure Bedalia could really end this fun park ride, no matter whether she was a witch or an angel. Why shouldn't she take her up on that? The voices stopped. Fog plugged her ears with silence. What would happen to her, to the baby? Was she the kind of woman who would walk away just because it was a little hard and very weird?

Emily's arms were hugging the mainmast, her head swaying side to side with the ship. Up this high, the rocking movement of the ship was amplified. She held on and clenched her eyes shut, trying to block out the strangeness and nausea.

"If that is what you wish."

27

"No," Emily said quietly, her eyes still tightly closed, hot tears stinging,

"I'm staying here, staying with my family, with this baby." It felt so good to say that. The words washed over her soul and gave her clarity of feeling she hadn't had before.

She opened her eyes to a black starry sky. The fog was gone; a breeze was again softly luffing the sails, the ship far from land and rocks. Slowly Emily climbed back down the ropes, easier now that she could see what she was doing. Maggie waited for her on the deck.

"Who were you shouting at?"

"You wouldn't believe me if I told you." Emily wondered if her face told of the weirdness she had just experienced.

"Try me."

They found a dark corner at the bow and leaned against the railing, shoulders touching. Emily told her mother the story of the visions on the mast.

"I think I'm going to keep this baby." And if that is what this whole dream is about, I should wake up tomorrow safe in my bed, on land.

CHAPTER THREE

....

MARY

Mary watched as Emily walked out of the storage room, as had the prior twelve women. Each of the women had stepped out from the tea shop onto the deck of the ship with a look of surprise, fear, and Mary thought, more than a little intrigue. It was clear that they had all inherited her late husband's sense of adventure.

Her father, a wealthy plantation owner who desired more wealth and power, had arranged her marriage to Blackbeard without her consent. It had been a short marriage, filled with violence from beginning to end. When Lieutenant Maynard, of the Virginia Navy, sailed into nearby waters and laid siege to Blackbeard's sloop the good lieutenant couldn't know the independence he was handing to Mary. Blackbeard died as he lived, by the pistol and sword.

It would have been just a bad memory if she hadn't been pregnant with his child. With Blackbeard dead, the child was the only tangible connection to the horror that was her marriage, and she was extremely happy to hand it over immediately after birth.

As that event was for her only some six months ago it was difficult to comprehend when that child, all grown up and having had a child of her own walked out of the storage closet as the first crew member. Ann was a perfect blend of Mary's fair complexion and Blackbeard's dark hair and eyes. There had not been much time to talk as Bedalia took the ship forward another generation and out walked Ann's child, all grown up. By the time all the women had been picked up Mary was accustomed to the closing darkness and squeeze on her chest that drove the air from her.

Once they had collected the last of her descendants, Bedalia had magicked the ship back to 1719 where they started. As soon as Mary's head was clear she gathered herself up as tall as she could and put as much gravity into her young voice as possible.

"Welcome aboard. I know this ship isn't much to look at, but it is strong and not so big that we can't sail her. I named her Maryann, for my name and my mother's. I see it is also the name of my daughter," she held her hand out to Ann, who reluctantly took it.

"Where are we?" one of the women asked.

"You are in the Caribbean Sea," answered Bedalia. She had moved from the bell over to the knot of women.

"What! How did that happen?" another asked.

"You have been brought here to help us, help Mary find a treasure." Mary detected the hesitation in Bedalia's voice. The women had agreed to help her, in fact, much of the plan was Bedalia's idea, yet Mary had not figured out why the mysterious Irish woman would want to help her.

"That sounds fun," someone at the back of the group said. Mary wondered if they were all so eager. A few looked positively terrified as if they would explode at any moment. Seconds later her thoughts were confirmed.

"Are you all crazy, I want to go home, now!" The speaker was a woman dressed in a long dress with a prim bustle at the back. Mary looked at the slim, dark-haired woman in the white and black dress. It was more narrowly styled than Mary's bustled and hooped skirt. Must be English, the French would never go for something so plain.

Emily stepped forward from the group and looking past Bedalia made eye contact with Mary. Mary felt a bolt of energy shoot between them. Emily's voice was calm and measured.

"Let me see if I understand this. We're on a ship that has traveled through time to pick up crew members who all are descendants of you, and we are to find a treasure. Is that it?"

"Yes, that neatly sums it up."

"So, who is Bedalia?" Emily turned her direct gaze to the woman.

"I'll let Bedalia tell her own story - Bedalia, please?"

Even on this filthy old boat in a cove a million miles from civilization Mary sounded like she was introducing someone at a garden party. Bedalia looked as if telling her story was the last thing in the world she wanted to do, but she took a slow deep breath and began her story.

"Long before any of you was born, I was a young woman myself. I loved the sea and wanted to sail more than life itself, but no ships would take me. Hiding my sex wasn't possible." She gestured to her ample bosom and smiled. A couple of the women nodded in recognition, stealing a glance at their own chests.

"I eventually found a ship, a merchant vessel captained by a certain Captain Hornigold. Soon after I joined a new crew member came aboard, a dashing young man named Edward Teach. He'd sailed from his home in England and like me wanted to find his life on the sea. Polished and well-read he was, a real British gentleman, different from anyone I had ever met. I fell in love. Of course, if I didn't show this, it wouldn't have been safe.

Emily looked around at the other women. They sat with their arms around their knees in rapt attention. As if the story had a magical hold on them.

"In no time Ed, the Captain, and I were thick as thieves. One night over a bottle of rum we decided to go after the treasure of Captain Henry Morgan. It was rumored that he raided Panama City, a city said to have great Spanish wealth stored in its vaults. He loaded up his men and mules to haul the treasure back to his ship. Some say he thought his sponsor, the Queen of England, wouldn't know the size of the booty, so he hid half in a cave on a small island. Planned to go back. The rest he took on to the Queen. But Morgan played a trick on his crew and sailed randomly for a month after leaving the island. By the time they reached England none of his crew could find their way back. Morgan died before he could mount an expedition to retrieve it. The rumors of the treasure had been around for decades, and Ed thought he knew where the island was. The three of us took a fast sloop out to where the spot was. Searched the island but didn't find the treasure. I'm convinced Ed was right and it's still there. He made a map."

"When we couldn't find the treasure, we quarreled. Ed and Hornigold argued about who should keep the map and shots were fired. I didn't join in but there wasn't anywhere to hide. A bullet went through my heart and I died there on the little island. Ed went on to become Blackbeard, feared by all on the high seas, Hornigold settled on Bahamas Island, or so he said."

Her voice went soft. "I still love him, but his connection with that treasure is too strong. He's trapped here in this world; unless that bond breaks, he will be doomed to stay here forever. If you can find the treasure and take it for yourselves, it'll allow him to let go. He can join me and together we can leave this world. That is why I'm helping Mary, but in truth, I'm helping myself."

The women sat in stunned silence. A treasure and a love affair. Two women connected to the same man. Isadora was the first to snap out of the reverie. Her father was a lawyer and had taught his daughter to be skeptical of everything.

"That is a sad story and likely a fairy tale made up to get us to go along with your plot. How could you be dead and still sitting here telling us this story?"

"I believe I'm still here in this plane to help Edward Teach redeem himself and be able to move on, to heaven or hell whichever it will be, but with me."

Mary could tell Izzie wasn't buying the story and was about to launch into another round of questioning that Bedalia couldn't answer, so she jumped in.

"The map is real." She pulled the map out of a pocket in her dress and spread it out on top of a nearby wooden box. The women crowded around. In the center of a yellowed parchment was an hourglass-shaped island with an x on it.

"Where did you get this?" Emily asked.

"Well, that is a bit of a story." Mary carefully refolded the map and slid it back into her pocket. Then she settled herself down cross-legged on the ship's deck. The others followed her lead. The deck rocked slowly on the calm waters of the cove, the sky still a bright robin's egg blue with white storm clouds forming on the horizon.

"I was sitting at my dressing table combing my hair. My mother taught me to brush one hundred strokes a day with the boar's hair brush to keep it glowing. As the daughter of a powerful plantation owner, I was expected to be ravishing as a reflection of the power of my father. It was just Daddy and me, and he managed my life."

34

Mary's stomach tightened at this thought. From her experience, women were only slightly above the slaves that were bought and sold on the docks and that position seemed tenuous at times. The chains on women were not links of iron; instead, they were restrictions on education, dictums to remain silent no matter how badly the men behaved, and taciturn acceptance of a husband and place in society as dictated by their fathers.

"If my mother had lived through childbirth with what would have been, should have been, my little brother, she would have helped me, I know it," Mary spoke more to herself than her listeners, "but she's dead. The baby wasn't strong enough to survive and one death became two."

"It is sadly more common than it should be, and men remarry as quickly as possible, to provide a governess, if nothing else, for the children. My father did not remarry though, choosing instead to focus his energy on building his power base in the colony. My father used me as a tool to expand his power, putting me out front as a host at parties, bartering with men over my hand, yet holding out on a marriage arrangement because it would not serve his purposes. I paid it all as little attention as possible. I couldn't change it."

"My father wanted more power and saw a pathway in the lucrative pirate trade. These shady transactions were 'on account,' the polite way of describing the mutual dealing between pirate and sponsor. He claimed not to know how the pirates came to have the goods they sold and from which he profited so much, but I knew how the pirates filled their holds with rum, cloths, furniture, and sugar, and I'm fairly sure my father knew as well."

"I remember the day my father told me he'd promised me in marriage to Blackbeard, the most notorious pirate of them all, as an incentive for him to stay in Bath and settle. My own father sold me into a form of slavery to a brutish man I detested. I'm sorry Bedalia, I know you love him, but I did not. The only positive I could find in the marriage was that Blackbeard, or Edward Teach, was under thirty years old. Most of the men my father toyed with as potential husbands were easily in their fifties or sixties, ancient and decrepit! According to gossip, Blackbeard wanted to settle down and enjoy a respectable life, having grown tired of running from the law. The wedding was just after my 16th birthday."

She took a deep breath and rearranged her skirts.

"At first Blackbeard's visits were nightly and it was with huge relief when his visits began to wane, and his sailings increased" She paused, then a slip of a smile graced her lips.

"I suspected that the quiet life of a gentleman wasn't what he had expected, and he had grown bored. It didn't lessen my fear. Locking my windows hadn't kept him out, and even when he didn't physically appear, he invaded my dreams leaving me curled in a ball beneath sheets and blankets despite the heat, trying to make myself as invisible as possible. If he did enter the room, he wouldn't see me hiding amongst the coverings."

"The night before he died, he came into my room as quietly as a cat, through an open balcony door. I don't know how long he stood watching me. I just know that I became aware of his presence when he moved into the light. I purposefully didn't look at his face, but I could see that he held something in his hand. He walked slowly over to my dressing table and placed a long metal key next to my hand mirror. He cleared his throat to speak and in a formal tone of voice said,

"The Governor of Virginia has sent ships and men to kill me. I don't think they will succeed," he hesitated, and I thought I detected doubt in his voice, "however…in the event my ship is sunk I want you to hold this for me, for safekeeping."

I couldn't move and I dared not breathe.

"It is a key to a tower, in St. Thomas," he explained, "should you need to use it, remember, twenty-six by five."

I nodded, not looking up. I didn't want to meet the coal-black eyes that harbored so much potential for violence. I had no idea what he was talking about with the riddle but wasn't about to ask. The longer he was here the greater the chance that he would touch me and violate me again. The last time had been very rough, and I had cried for days. Worse still, I was beginning to feel strange, queasy, and lightheaded."

Mary paused and looked over at Ann, hoping her daughter was beginning to understand why she had given her up.

"Frozen to my seat, I heard Blackbeard grunt, turn, and walk out the balcony door. I sat like that for five minutes after he left, afraid that if I moved, he would come back. When I was sure he wouldn't, I slowly crept over and locked the door. That done I

37

walked back to my dressing table and picked up the key. It was long, made of rough iron, and had the initials ET scratched on the side. ET for Edward Teach. For you see, I am Mary Teach, wife of Blackbeard the pirate, and you are all my decedents."

CHAPTER FOUR

EMILY

Emily sat listening to Mary's quiet voice tell of her marriage to Blackbeard and thinking about her own situation. She had gotten herself 'in trouble,' a phrase she'd heard her mother use to describe girls who were unwed and pregnant. It didn't seem to matter that the tabloids were full of stars that had children out of wedlock. To her mother, that meant the woman was in trouble.

At least she wasn't being forced to marry someone she didn't like, or know, and didn't have to deal with that on top of her pregnancy.

Pregnant. It had such a final sound to it. As in, "I'm pregnant and the world will change – my life will change, I can't do what I had planned to do with my life." Emily's mind raced, repeating, what am I going to do? over and over and over. How could I have been so stupid, to let myself get pregnant?

Mary's story was almost bigger than life and explained how she had come to be the wife of Blackbeard, but not how she came to have the map.

"Mary, the map, how did you find the map?" Maggie asked, interrupting. Mary nodded.

"I'm getting there," she paused for a moment longer and then continued her story. "News of the battle traveled fast. The first shots were fired at dawn in Ocracoke Inlet, and I was awakened by my maid as the muffled sounds drifted on the morning breezes into town. I dressed quickly, choosing a yellow dress because the color makes me happy, and wrapped a white crocheted shawl my aunt made around my shoulders. The waistband on my dress felt a bit tighter than the last time I had worn it and looking back that was the first clue that I was pregnant. In my heart of hearts, I hoped the Governor of Virginia was successful in his quest. Marriage to Blackbeard had been a nightmare and I was anxious to awake and find it over. Ridding the town of the pirates would bring back a level of civil calm once the trauma had drifted far enough into the past for life to return to some level of normal."

"I considered riding out to watch the battle, to see for myself whether the Governor's men would save me from the fate my own father had dealt me. Fear held me back though, as it would have been dangerous; cannons are notoriously unpredictable and difficult to aim. I stood on the main street, along with other town's people, straining to see flashes of light from the cannon fire, though I knew they were too far away and the morning light too bright to see anything. The west blowing breezes brought the acrid smell of gun powder mingled with the sweet smell of gardenias and tulip."

"The battle lasted barely an hour when the guns went silent, the fresh sea breezes clearing the smoke that lingered among the tulip trees. Finally, young boys mounted horses and rode out to get a report. Of course, those of us with any sense I our heads stayed rooted to the cobbled roads, whispering, The boys returned some thirty minutes later, out of breath, shouting. That Blackbeard was dead. Not just dead, but beheaded. His ship was going down in flames in the shallow water and his men, those left alive, were captured."

Mary paused and Emily thought she looked lost in the happiness of that one moment when her tormenter was dead. Taking a breath, she continued,

"I gathered my skirts and walked slowly back to the house. I was careful not to look at anyone as I walked and even more careful not to smile. Once safely in my room I was laughing and crying at the same time. I was a widow at sixteen and glad of it. I remember sitting at my dressing table and picking up the key, running my fingers up and down the shaft. It was dark, cold, and smooth; hand tempered, and with an eerie foreboding feeling that ran through my hand, arm, and body. What was in the tower I wondered? What didn't Blackbeard want them to find?

The answer would have to wait though, as a wave of nausea welled up inside me."

Mary stopped talking. Her eyes were looking down at her fingers, twisting a loose thread from her skirt.

"Eight months later a child was born and immediately whisked off to another family. I'm afraid my memories of Blackbeard and his violence had erased any maternal instinct I had been capable of, and I reasoned that since I had not wanted the marriage or the child in the first place, it didn't exist. I didn't even see the child after I gave birth; preferring to think it had either died or hadn't existed in the first place."

Mary looked over at Ann, who listened intently.

"I'm so sorry Ann, though I know words can't make it right." Tears filled her eyes. Ann looked away.

"I refused to wear black in mourning, which caused many tongues to wag, but otherwise I played the role of the bereaved widow, giving me privileges I had not expected. I was shocked to learn from the Governor's wife that some of the town's residents had thought that I loved Blackbeard and mourned his passing. How could they have been so blind? Couldn't they see the effect he was having on me and everyone else in town? I put these sentimental beliefs to clever use though; when I made it known that I wished to sail to St. Thomas to collect my late husband's belongings. I wanted to see why that key was so important to him that he made sure it didn't go down with his ship. It was an outlandish request. Women don't sail to islands alone. They may sail to England or France, in the company of an older gentleman, who would escort her, but not to notorious pirate hangouts. I played up my desire to follow in my dead husband's footsteps, see what his life away from me was like, and collect mementos of him. No one batted an eye," Mary laughed,

"Even my father, who finally seemed to have realized the pain he had inflicted seemed willing to indulge me. He arranged passage on a southbound merchant ship, and I left a fortnight later, the gold coins he had given me were wrapped tightly around my waist, under the new yellow, bustled dress I wore, the latest fashion from Paris. I traveled unescorted, yet under the watchful eye of the ship's captain, Donald Cameron, a longtime friend of my father. The captain owed my father a large favor and I'm sure it was only that debt that kept him from entering my cabin at night."

Mary shifted her legs, straightening them out and then tucking them both up to the left. She smoothed her dress across her lap and finding the loose thread again carefully broke it off. The crew watched her actions, and no one spoke.

Emily tried to imagine herself in Mary's place. The progress made by the women's movement in the sixties and seventies had made such a journey unremarkable. Women traveled alone frequently and spring break in the Caribbean was practically a religion. Mary spoke with a refined tone and language that sounded foreign to Emily's ear, even though the words were English.

Finally looking up Mary continued, "The sea invigorated me, filling my dreams at night with white sails and dancing sun rays. I had never felt so free in my life and for the first time I thought I had a small insight into Blackbeard's love of the sea. The exhilaration of the water when it splashed up, the power of the sails full of wind as they drove the ship forward; all gave me chills. For a young woman raised in the civilized society of the colonies, this was forbidden. I felt such as I had never felt before."

"I found a spot on the deck railing that kept me out of the crew's way and stood there all day, day after day, coming in only for food and rest. The ship made many ports, as we sailed south from the Carolinas, and with each port, my delight grew. The world was so much bigger and more colorful than little Bath Township, where I had spent my whole life. Dolphins swam alongside the ship, jumping playfully out of the water as if to entertain me and beckon me to join them. They blended into the water so quickly that I had trouble tracking them as they swam, just under the surface, and leaped for joy a few yards out.

As the ship sailed south and made stops at islands in the Caribbean waters, I began to see the brown-skinned people. Before this, my only exposures to skin of any other color than my own were the slaves that worked on my father's plantation. Here they were not slaves, but shop owners, sailors, and cooks. They interacted with the men on the merchant ship as equals. I entered a bigger world, so much more real than the world I had known, filled with all types of people, speaking all types of languages, and wearing all types of clothes. I began to have a strange recurring dream about a tea shop and an Irish woman with multicolored clothes. It wasn't a woman I had met up to that point, but now I know it was Bedalia. She was contacting me in my dreams."

"After two months on the sea, the ship docked at a long wooden dock in the town of Charlotte Amalie. The air was warm and damp. Everyone I asked knew where Blackbeard's tower was, perched on a hill to the northeast of town with a view of the harbor mouth, opening to the Caribbean Sea. It was not the best-kept secret if it had been a secret at all. The tower is tall and narrow, like a chess rook, made of square stone blocks, with a solid wooden door on the north side. The weathered, wooden door had thick iron hinges, a pounded metal strap, and a round iron medallion with a keyhole in the center. Rumors of a treasure were rampant, so I'm sure the help I received from three roughnecks wasn't out of the goodness of their hearts. Their worn and torn britches and soiled gray tunics told me louder than words what type of men they were, pirates, but I needed help.

The climb up the hill was long, hot, and dusty and we all arrived at the top of the hill out of breath. The heat and humidity were taking their toll on me. I was dressed in a beautiful pale blue, tight-waist shirtdress, laced and buttoned up the front. It was the latest fashion from London, or so the captain of the ship who transported it over to the colonies had told my father. Underneath I wore pantaloons and an underskirt of the prettiest lace and silk. I did not need to wear the dreaded corset that older women wore to cinch in their waists.

"As you can see," she indicated the light dress she was wearing, "I've learned my lesson. One must dress for the climate regardless of what the fashion in Paris or London is." She again smoothed the light cotton dress, un-corseted and pale yellow. Emily saw that Mary had her audience entranced and didn't want to lose being the center of attention. She enjoyed the limelight.

After a long pause, Mary continued.

"The sailors waited patiently behind me as I pulled out the long metal key from the small handbag I had tied around my waist. The key slipped in the lock smoothly, and the large wooden door swung with a shriek from the salt corroded iron hinges scraping across rust. It was dark inside. Dank air rushed out. The cool air felt good, and I made to move inside when they rushed up behind me, pushed me to the ground, and ran in."

CHAPTER FIVE

EMILY

Emily listened, mesmerized by the story unfolding. She couldn't help it, seeing Mary sitting there telling how she sailed as a woman, alone as it were, for two months on a boat only to arrive at an island and be attacked by pirates. She had done this all wearing a dress Emily couldn't imagine even getting into. Emily looked down at her khaki pants and blue, button-down shirt, the outfit she wore every day to work. She had the same shirt in yellow, white, and pink, but it was blue that blended in best with the men. Her profession as a marine engineer meant she too spent her days in a male environment, and her approach had been to blend in as much as possible, to not really come across as a woman, but as one of the boys.

Of course, that option never occurred to Mary. Women dressed as women; men dressed like men. She looked up as Mary continued.

"I was getting to my feet, and brushing weeds off when the three pirates emerged, glowered at me, and stomped off. At that point I realized how lucky I was that they had not attacked me, given that I was alone. I think that they must have feared Blackbeard, even in death, and decided that raping me would bring upon their heads more grief than I was worth.

Once I was convinced the pirates were gone, I slowly entered the cool darkness. I'm not sure what I expected but the tower was a single, high vaulted room. In the middle of the room, which was not more than thirty feet wide, was a large carved wooden chair, a dusty lantern, and a pile of books. A small cot was off to the side. arrow, slit windows cut into the walls, just high enough and wide enough for a man to point a musket out. These windows didn't allow in much light, but it was enough to see that there was no treasure in the tower."

"Weren't you scared?" asked Winnie. Mary shook her head.

"No, I was more surprised than anything. Surprised the tower was so small, surprised by the chair, and mostly surprised by the pile of books. Blackbeard the pirate didn't strike me as a reading man."

Bedalia spoke. "He was educated at Cambridge. It was only his birth order that prevented him from becoming a government minister. Third sons are not considered for these types of things."

"He never mentioned anything about his family to me. Anyway, I picked up the top book, and read the author's name.

Chaucer. The wick on the lantern still looked useable, and so I pulled out a small flint from my handbag and lit the lamp, thinking over and over, what did he mean by twenty-six by five?"

"You had flint in your handbag! Whatever made you think of having that?" Sophia asked.

"I was exploring, of course, so I carried things I didn't usually have. Besides the flint, I had a small pistol, which I have fortunately not had to use, yet." She seemed quite proud of her independence and cleverness.

"I returned each day to sit in that carved wooden chair, with its turned legs and carved leather stretched across the back, repeating to myself, "twenty-six by five" and reading the books. It is a beautiful chair, with a solid seat, a tattered cushion, and carved decorations on the sides of the seat pan with floral patterns. I recognized it as a rosewood chair because I had seen a similar chair in my father's office."

"After six days of sitting in that chair, savoring the cool darkness, and staring at the curved walls something occurred to me. The tower was constructed with twenty-five rows of stone blocks, one on top of each other, making the walls.

There were ninety-four blocks in the circumference. The twenty-sixth block around, starting at the door, in the fifth row, was different from the rest. It stuck out slightly more than the others. Reaching up I was able to move it slightly when I tugged on it, and with hundreds of little back-and-forth motions, I was able to free it from the wall.

49

The piece that came out was not the thickness of the wall. It was only about five inches thick. Despite that, it was heavy, and when finally released from the wall it landed in my hands and I fell backward landing hard on the dirt floor of the tower." Mary absentmindedly rubbed her lower back as she relived the fall, making a face that made everyone laugh.

"I noticed that the piece I held had a hollowed-out portion and laying, neatly folded in the indentation was a piece of parchment paper. Opening it I could see it was a map, this map." Mary patted the pocket of her dress where the map hid, safely tucked away.

"So, all we have to do is follow the map, find the treasure and somehow return to our own time," Isadora said.

"Yes, that's it."

"I believe you will not be alone in your hunt for the treasure." Everyone turned to look at Bedalia.

"I believe Hornigold is after it too. He's been looking for an opportunity to go back, but he doesn't have the map. He'll know Mary is out looking for it; people talk. We will have to avoid him, which may prove difficult. He is ruthless and he'll kill you all without a second thought."

At this first hint of real danger, silence enveloped the group. It seemed to Emily that none of them were breathing, and she herself was holding her breath.

"We could die? How does that work, I mean technically I haven't been born yet, so how could I get killed? Does that mean I would never be born?" Everyone looked at Bedalia for an answer.

"Death is relative," Bedalia answered, "you have all already been born and that will not change." If she thought this would be reassuring it most definitely was not.

Emily moaned, "I don't like the sound of that."

"What do we do next?" Mary asked Bedalia.

"Start sailing, and I suggest doing some cleaning and maintenance on this ship."

Emily looked around at the wooden ship with a practiced eye. It was clearly incredibly old or built to look that way. The style was Dutch, usually called a Dutch Fleut. She had studied the designs in a navel marine history class.

The Fleut was a broad, flat-bottomed boat that became the prototype for modern cargo carriers because it could carry 50 percent more cargo than other designs of its time. It was a strong ship about the size of two motorhomes parked end to end. Inexpensive to build and could be sailed with a twelve-person crew. A tall mast, around four feet in diameter, towered into the sky. Sails hung from the topmost yardarms

The ship strained against the anchor chain. She was sure she had seen this place before in her dreams. She often dreamed of sailing vessels, it was one reason she had become a marine engineer, and the recurrence of the scene before her made her more convinced she was dreaming.

Contemplating the next step, Emily looked around the circle of women. Each face was like hers in a way that she couldn't quite put her finger on, a slightly different hair color maybe or rounder eyes, or hazel rather than blue eyes. The women arrived clothed in an impressive collection of period outfits, ranging from tight shirtwaist dresses with enormous hoop skirts to lime green pedal pushers from the 1960s It was as if a Hollywood costume shop had been raided. No one spoke, and the music of the ropes on the mast as the ship rocked slowly at anchor was the only soundtrack. The creaking of the wood and slapping of the ropes on the sails had a rumba beat.

Mary clapped her hands. "Well let's get started. First, we need to get into some different clothes. One of these crates contains tunics and pants. They will be more comfortable than the dresses most of us wear."

She looked at Emily in her khaki work slacks and a blue, button-down shirt. Winnie was sitting on a box, so she hopped off and pried the lid off the nearest crate. She held up the tunic lying at the top.

Made of a plain white broadcloth material it looked serviceable if not fashionable. Winnie made a face as she looked at the shapeless top. Emily would learn that Winnie loved clothes and was proud to say she made all her own dresses.

"I think we can dress these up a bit," she said as she tossed the first tunic to Caroline who was sitting closest. Once everyone had changed into the new tunic and pants, Mary divided the group into three sub-teams. One team, the one Emily joined, headed off to find cleaning materials. Another team started off looking for repair equipment, and the third team headed to the main mast where Bedalia taught them how to run up the net of ropes to adjust the sails.

"Ask Henry for help finding the cleaning solutions," Mary called out as they headed down below the top deck.

"Who's Henry?" Emily asked, pausing at the entrance. Henry was not a name that had come up in any of Mary's stories. Emily was sure she had not seen a man since she had boarded the ship. If boarding was what you could call how she'd gotten here.

"Jesh, Mary, how many more surprises do you have in store for us, I'm not sure I can handle any more weirdness." Mary smiled and shrugged as if to say - who knows? Emily shook her head and turned around. This must be a dream, I'm sure being dead makes more sense than this.

Emily and her team headed below to the galley.

Despite the brightness of the light on deck, it got dark as she walked carefully down the wooden steps which sounded like they couldn't hold much more than a feather in weight. They found the galley and an area where hammocks were hung between poles, swinging gently with the ship. The galley was small, with a wooden table set on top of barrels, full of foodstuffs. A cast-iron stove and low shelves stuffed with old bowls and spoons ran along one side. Sitting on a wooden bench was a dark-haired man with a patch over one eye. He looked vaguely familiar.

53

"Hello."

The one-eyed man looked up from the carving he was working on. He used a large blade that hardly looked suitable to carve the intricate detail it nevertheless was carving.

"I'm Emily."

"Henry's my name I'll be helping Mary and the rest of you."

"Helping us! Good, you can start by helping us find something to clean the filth on this ship." Henry pointed with his blade to a crate. Caroline walked over and rummaged around. after a few minutes, she held up a glass jug of clear liquid.

"Vinegar," Henry grunted, "that'll do." The team grabbed some bowls and the vinegar and headed up to the top deck. Henry followed them without a sound.

The maintenance team had also returned to the top deck, and they had some extra wood, a planer, sanding papers, and marine varnish. This ship may be old, Emily thought, but it's going to be clean and well maintained. The key to a successful voyage is a sound ship.

CHAPTER SIX

EMILY

They spent the next few hours cleaning and repairing as the sun rose higher in the sky until eventually, the air grew too hot to even move. Henry had pitched in and proven himself to be useful. As the heat rose, work stopped and the sails hung limply as the women sat on the deck, in shade created by draping old sails over the yardarms and railings, on ropes and on barrels, and told their stories.

Henry faded into the background. It was like hearing a verbal history book of accomplished women through the ages. Emily learned that her family had lived through all the momentous events that defined the history of the new nation, and she listened with growing interest as the birth dates grew nearer to her own.

Her great grandmother, Caroline, had been born in 1915, was adopted into a Catholic family, had studied to be a doctor, and gave birth to an illegitimate child in 1935. Emily could see that she had inherited the same auburn hair and blue eyes as Caroline. She had a warm, soft voice and Emily could tell she would have the right bedside manner for dealing with new mothers. Caroline's own child, a baby girl, was adopted by a nice couple from Florida, and Caroline became the first female physician in Shreveport, Louisiana. That she bore no more children, despite a long happy marriage to Charles Glover was seen by some as the price a woman must pay for a career outside the home. Her specialty was obstetrics, and despite delivering hundreds of other women's babies, she never sought out her own, such was her shame.

She looked down at her hands as she told her story, occasionally wiping away the tears that flowed down her cheeks. When she was composed again, she lifted her head and scanned the group, eventually settling on Emily. Their eyes locked and Emily was certain that her great grandmother, using ob-gyn intuition honed through decades, had sensed she was pregnant. An unnerving sense of time settled over Emily.

This woman spoke as if she had lived her entire life and died, yet as Emily followed the timeline, her great grandmother had been born in 1915 and the ship was in 1719. That would mean that technically Caroline hadn't been born yet. Looking around this seemed the case for most of the women. Emily thought there was a metaphysical theory about this that hadn't been covered in her engineering curriculum or a Star Trek episode because she couldn't think of one technical theory that helped. Yet there they all were. It could be a dream, the sailing ship was familiar, but she could see faces and hear the stories, and that was not like any dream she'd ever had. Or it could be the tea.

Caroline's only child, a baby girl, and Emily's grandmother grew up in the progressive city of Miami Beach, the daughter of a lawyer and his socialite wife. They named her Isadora, Izzie to her girlfriends. She had a flair for cooking and life. She loved to party and had lots of friends. Her green eyes penetrated your soul, causing people to confess things to her spontaneously and unbidden. A calling as a psychiatrist seemed natural, but her heart latched on to cooking and she was well on her way to sous chef at a four-star restaurant when a moment of indiscretion with a busser at the restaurant led to pregnancy.

Horrified, her parents sent her away to stay with cousins in North Carolina, sufficiently far enough away to prevent gossip, to have the child. Izzie had the baby and discretely handed her over to an adoption agency her father had arranged. She returned home rested, and the sous chef position was hers. After a time, she opened her own restaurant.

Izzie's eyes laughed as she spoke, her zest for life not leaving any place for tears over decisions made or events passed. She alone didn't seem too bothered that her daughter, a human being she hadn't given much thought to after a difficult delivery, was sitting across from her, watching her every movement.

Izzie's daughter, Margaret, was adopted by a very wealthy couple in the hopes that a child would save their marriage, which it didn't. Margaret's adopted mother didn't want to carry her own

57

child as it would have ruined her figure, a feature she highlighted in glimmering ball gowns at all the social events they attended.

The addition of Margaret did not prevent the divorce that had been brewing and she was raised by a nanny, rarely seeing her adopted mother. She gave up her own baby at her mother's insistence, as keeping it would have soiled the family name. Before handing the child over to the adoption agency she printed the name Emily, after Emily Dickinson her favorite author, on a slip of paper and tucked it into the blankets.

Margaret went on to become a lawyer, drawn inexplicably to maritime law. She made partner in an age when law firms were unaccustomed to female lawyers. She eventually married an older man from the social circle her mother favored and was miserable, despite much wealth.

Emily was coming to realize that even if she gave up the baby she carried, she wanted a relationship with it, so it knew its birth mother.

IT. Why did she think of the baby growing inside her as an IT? It had to be a boy or a girl. Looking at the crew of women sitting around talking about their lives she realized – of course, it would be a girl.

The sea remained calm that day, the air was hot and still. As the sun began to drop behind the rocky hills surrounding the cove and the temperature started to drop, the crew began working again.

Isadora went down the wooden stairs to the little galley and began to rummage around for food to make dinner.

On deck, Bedalia opened one of the wooden crates to reveal swords, with long broad steel blades. She picked up the top sword and then everyone was invited to take a one.

'Swords, good lord these are real swords,' Emily thought as she picked up the metal blade and moving away from the group began to swing it. It was heavy and clumsy. She could tell her arm was going to be very sore. Bedalia too began to swing a sword, back and forth rhythmically, making it look as easy as swinging a small tree branch. She had a practiced swing, purposeful and strong and Emily tried to mimic her movements. After distributing all the swords, Bedalia demonstrated a few movements. Slow, deliberate movements that focused on form and strength.

Emily took to the sword as if she were born to it, as indeed they all had been, for each of them had the blood of a feared sea pirate coursing through her veins. After an hour of swordplay, which was all they could handle, Bedalia gathered them together and talked about the ropes, how the sails were attached and managed, what the various rigging configurations were called, and how to adjust them to catch or release the wind. She proved to be quite an experienced sailor and a good teacher. Emily's arms ached by the end of the day.

The sun seemed to linger in the sky as if the gods had directed it not to set until the crew learned to sail the wooden ship and wield a sword. At last, with the women exhausted, the sun dropped below the horizon, the sky marking the event with a darkening towards indigo and the clouds on the horizon capturing the lingering light with splashes of pink and coral.

The meal Isadora dished out from the meager kitchen was hearty and fresh. Emily was so tired that eating shoe leather would have satisfied her, but Isadora ensured they had a real gourmet meal. After their meal, the women returned to the top deck to breathe the fresh air and continue talking, breaking into smaller groups or just one on one.

A crescent sliver of moon hung in the sky, which slowly came alive with an explosion of stars. A gentle, warm breeze stirred as the women found places to sit or lean on deck, close their eyes, and savor the moment before heading below again to crawl into the woven hammocks awaiting each of them.

"Is this real do you suppose?" Winnie asked.

"I don't see how it could be," answered Maggie, "but it's a fun dream anyway."

"I'm not sure this is a dream." Emily rubbed her arms. "In dreams, muscles don't ache, and mine ache from swinging that sword. On the other hand, in real life, we all couldn't be here, so I'm not sure what to make of it. We don't seem to be in any danger, so real or not I'm going to roll with it."

CHAPTER SEVEN

MARY

Mary chose a spot on a large crate and pulled her legs up cross-legged fashion in front of her. The feel of the capris on her legs was still strange, and she enjoyed the freedom of not wearing a tight-waist, floor-length dress.

At parties, she had heard women talking about Anne Bonney and Mary Reid, two women who had broken convention by dressing as men and sailing as pirates. Their story was whispered quietly away from the men, their bravery admired and their success at escaping the bonds of society envied. They would have dressed much as she was now in pants and a tunic. Their breasts would be bound though, a sacrifice she and her crew did not need to make.

The sailing, sword-play lessons, and a satisfying meal had loosened some of the reserve among the women, and mothers and daughters were beginning to describe their lives, laughing, and crying at the same time.

The girl named Elaine stood. "Who exactly is Bedalia? Her story was entertaining but too fantastic to be real." Elaine had shared that she was a poet and romantic story writer. Of course, she would find something as fanciful as Bedalia's story a fabrication. Just the sort of fabrication she would make up as a writer.

Mary looked around to see if the strange woman was on deck. After teaching the sword and ropes all day she had vanished.

"Well, I'm not sure how to explain it, and I'm not really sure myself, but I think she is some sort of a witch."

"Or an angel…," offered Elaine.

As the moon crept over the steel grey horizon, the women slowly drifted below deck to their hammocks and a night of well-deserved sleep. Mary remained, watching them leave. She had taken the Captain's quarters as her own. It seemed a bit special, and she wasn't sure how her descendants would feel about it.

"Mary?" Ann stood to Mary's right, looking at the woman who was her mother. Mary turned to look at her. Her daughter had her eyes. Eyes that Mary thought were filled with distrust, and she couldn't blame her. Mary knew that the ship was bewitched and that through the magic of Bedalia all her daughters had been brought back from their own time. She had thought about it for quite some time before agreeing to do it to get the treasure. All her descendants were trying to understand it for the first time and would naturally distrust her and Bedalia. She didn't trust Bedalia either, her motives in helping Mary were not entirely clear.

"Yes, Ann."

"Listening to you describe Blackbeard, my father, I don't imagine you are very happy to see me."

"Well, I can imagine it sounds that way." Mary conceded, "It isn't so much that I didn't want you," she continued, "but more that I didn't want any symbols of him." Ann was quiet. She hates me, thought Mary.

"I'm sorry if life was, is, hard for you because of my decision."

"Life itself isn't so hard, my adoptive family loves me."

"I'm glad to hear that. Where do you live?" Mary wanted to put her arm around Ann but held back.

"That's the funny thing, I live in the same town that you do. I don't know how this all works, but I imagine that to you I'm much younger than I am now," Ann's voice trailed off.

"Do we know each other?"

"My parents are the Governor and his wife." Mary's mouth dropped open.

"Really!"

"But I don't think we've met, yet, if I followed the timeline correctly, I'm only about one year old."

"Well, yes, now you are, but soon you will be old enough, and perhaps we can figure out a way to be together." Mary's heart pounded. "Maybe we can even stay here until you are old enough to remember me when we get back."

"I don't think you can go back to being my mother."

"No, of course not, let's just get to know one another first."

Ann nodded her head, turned, and headed to the wooden steps.

"Ann?" Mary called out. Ann stopped and partially turned.

"I really am sorry." Ann continued down the stairs.

CHAPTER EIGHT

EMILY

Emily's hammock rocked, softly, from side to side, and the moon shone brightly down the stairway into the hold. The motion reminded her of the train ride she and her mother had taken last fall up to New York. The rhythm was soothing. It lulled her to a half-awake, half-dream state. What would her mother say when she found out her only daughter was pregnant? She would want to know what Emily planned to do. Emily was wondering the same thing. She ran over her conversation with Mark in her head. His voice had felt supportive, his words caring. He was nice looking, she wouldn't mind seeing him again, under better circumstances.

Emily felt a light tap on her shoulder. She looked up to see Maggie holding her finger over her mouth in a shushing manner, indicating they should be quiet. She was not lying in her bed on dry land, she was still in a dank old ship, laying in a rope hammock. Things didn't make any sense, if it wasn't a dream, then what was it? She looked around and saw other dark forms moving silently inside the ship's hold. It must be the middle of the night Emily thought and got up slowly. They quietly walked up to the top deck where the rest of the women were sitting in a circle. Emily and Maggie were the last to join the group.

Emily was surprised to see Bedalia sitting in the circle as well. In fact, she was such a bright presence that she was the link that held the necklace of women together, beginning and ending with Bedalia. Had it been just a few hours earlier that she had run into Bedalia, on the mizzen mast, assuming for the moment that had really happened at all, Emily had thought it was a dream, but now she wasn't sure. Most of her dreams didn't go on this long, and once a point was made, morphed into some other weird dream sequence. This just kept going.

Bedalia closed her eyes and began to hum, and as she hummed, she began to sway her upper body around and around. It was catching and soon the women around the circle were closing their eyes. No one hummed, but they were closing their eyes and seemed to join in the space Bedalia was creating. Emily closed her eyes last. A warm soft feeling, like a summer breeze, embraced her inside and out. Colors swam inside her head, swirling and curling with the humming.

Bedalia stopped humming. Emily could hardly hear her voice when she spoke. "You have heard the stories of each other. Tonight, I want you to close your eyes and think about the story of your mother and grandmother, and I want you to imagine yourself as your mother in her story." Then she fell silent.

Oh brother, thought Emily, this is like one of those spiritual cruises that I've read about in the travel magazines that my mother - my adopted mother gets.

"Put myself in Maggie's shoes, put myself in Maggie's shoes," she repeated over and over to herself. Emily visualized the woman that was sitting to her left. She had the same auburn hair as Emily, or it would be more accurate to say Emily had the same auburn hair as Maggie. Emily smiled as she looked at the whole picture of her mother, at herself dressed like her mother, being her mother. Suddenly she felt overwhelmed by a sense of guilt and fear that felt all too familiar. It was the very same feeling she'd been battling for the last weeks since realizing she was pregnant. Yet this was different, it wasn't Mark's child she was pregnant with, it was another man's child. Emily was aware enough in the visualization to realize that the child she was pregnant with was her and that this woman whom she was embodying, and visualizing, would give birth to this baby and would in turn give it up, would give her away, would give her to Emily's adopted parents.

"Part of becoming a woman is learning the conditions and history of your family and passing along the traditions. To do that you need your mother, your grandmother, to hold your hand through tough times, to tell you the successes and failures of the family, the traditions and culture that shaped the family. This family has not had that. The culture and traditions that have been passed along to you are not those of your blood family, not your successes and failures. That lack, that vacant space in your lives has

67

caused you to search for answers in places that didn't contain answers. It got you into trouble. With this voyage, you have a chance to heal. You have a chance to heal yourself; you have a chance to heal Edward Teach. Like it or not, Edward Teach is your ancestor and you owe him this," Bedalia's voice sounded firm. Scolding Emily couldn't argue with that, without Blackbeard, none of them would be sitting here in the first place.

"The traditions of the Teach family include his treasure and a habit of not taking responsibility for the things you've done."

Emily thought about the feelings of guilt and anguish she had sensed in her mother while visualizing being her, and she knew the same feelings for the child she was carrying. This was the legacy passed from mother to daughter in this family, abandon the product of your mistakes.

Mary squirmed. "I can't sit and listen to this anymore. Blackbeard certainly didn't set a good example for the rest of us to follow."

"Aye," Bedalia agreed, "but that doesn't mean you can't rise above him." Heads slowly nodded around the circle. Emily felt Bedalia's softly squeeze her hand and a charge of energy pass between them. Instinctively Emily squeezed Maggie's hand and slowly the squeeze began to move around the circle. When it reached Mary Emily could see her forbearer was reluctant to squeeze Bedalia's hand, yet eventually she did. Bedalia squeezed

Emily's hand again and the squeeze began around the circle, faster this time until it became a race to get it around as fast as possible.

The energy level in the group went up each time the squeeze made its way around and soon they were laughing boisterously as they tried to keep it going. Emily lost track of the number of times the squeeze went around the circle when she felt Bedalia pull her hand towards her and felt Mary's hand replace Bedalia's. The tea woman silently backed out of the circle, slipped into the shadows of the deck, and disappeared. Emily and Mary looked at each other, the alpha, and the omega, and realized without words that they were the links that kept the circle together. They would get this group to the treasure and back, Mary, who started the tradition, and Emily who could end it.

Exhaustion finally caught up with them and the circle began to break up as the women drifted back down to their hammocks to dream of the colorful energy that they had shared. Emily was too tired to sleep. She had never felt this level of knowledge within herself. Knowing where she fit in the world, knowing more of what was expected of her. I'm not really the omega she thought that distinction goes to my daughter, whom I'm going to name Grace.

Emily watched the water shimmer with starlight. Her mind went back over the experience she had just had. As she sat connected to the circle, she felt a part of something bigger than herself in a way no church ceremony could have ever done. Madeline came over and leaned on the railing next to Emily.

69

"Pretty, isn't it?"

"Yeah, it sure is," Emily agreed. Madeline's nose was the same as hers, but her hair was slightly darker.

"May I ask you a personal question?"

"Certainly, we're related after all."

"Why did you get married?"

Madeline pulled herself up to full height, her face set, and pulled down on her tunic. Emily feared she had insulted her. After a moment, she relaxed a bit and returned to leaning on the railing.

"Well, I really didn't have much choice, did I?" she said.

"I don't know, did you?" To Emily, the decision to marry was made for reasons of love.

"No, no I didn't. You either marry or get labeled a spinster, and in my family," she paused, "my adopted family, being a spinster wasn't acceptable. So, I married Walter, and no, before you ask, I don't love him. But he's rich, which does compensate somewhat."

"Have you ever loved someone?"

"Yes, I loved Caroline's father." Emily looked sideways at Madeline. She could tell the other woman was lost in a memory.

"His name was Eddie. Funny isn't it, how close that is to Ed Teach. He worked for my father at the ranch. When I got pregnant, they fired him. I don't know what words were said but Eddie left. I haven't seen him since."

"How did you know you were in love?"

70

Madeline smiled at Emily. Emily realized how stupid that question must have sounded.

"It's just, well, I'm not sure I've ever felt it," she explained.

"I wish I could say how you will know. I realized it over time, I missed him when he wasn't there, dreamed about him. It felt like my heart was clawed out of my chest when he left." Have you met someone you may love?" Emily thought of Mark. Could she love someone she had only really met? Her brain said no, she didn't know him well enough to love him. Her heart was saying yes as if its beating resonated with him and his alone.

"No, yes, oh I don't know." Madeline laughed.
"I see. Well, listen to your heart, it will tell you."

She patted Emily on the arm and turned to head to her hammock, leaving Emily to stare at the water and wonder if she was in love.

CHAPTER NINE

EMILY

On the seventh day, by Emily's counting, life onboard *The Maryann* had settled into a routine of training on the ropes, climbing up and down, letting the sails in and out. They spent hours conducting fake sword fights, swabbing the deck, to keep the wood wet and the boards swollen, polishing the brass fittings, which seemed to tarnish overnight in the salty air, and talking around the large wooden table in the galley about where the treasure might be.

Emily was getting comfortable with the idea that she had been transported back in time, as improbable as that seemed, and was on a ship with her relatives. As her doubt subsided, the idea of treasure invaded Emily's thoughts. Judging by the amount of conversation about it, the others were equally obsessed. She found talking about the treasure easier than trying to talk to her ancestors. There was a gap in the culture to bridge that included language and references. It was amazing how much the English language had changed in two hundred years. They were fourteen women connected by blood and disconnected by time. Henry alone seemed above it all. He hovered on the edges, not sharing who he was or why he was there.

She lay in her hammock that morning, listening to the sounds of cooking, cleaning, polishing, and the ever-present slap of the water against the hull. The hammock swayed side to side, the fibers squeaking quietly. How different from the sounds of her life up until now. She hadn't touched a computer in days, hadn't heard the insistent ding of the email system informing her yet another email had made its way to her inbox. She moved her wrists in circular motions, noticing that the persistent twinge was diminishing. The concept of a sweatshop had mostly vanished in the United States, setting aside illegal garment shops. What had replaced it though, were well-paying jobs working on computers all day and developing repetitive stress injuries that sapped strength and vitality out of one's body. Her company had done much to alleviate the potential for harm, but nothing could get around the fact that she spent most of her days chained to a computer responding to emails and creating charts and graphs.

The real design portion of her job seemed minuscule in comparison to keeping up with communication. Computers were supposed to simplify things and give us more free time, she mused, but in fact, they had done the opposite. More of life, in general, had transitioned into the little electronic boxes of amazing variety and the umbilical cord was strong, forcing us into automated bill paying computer links to our banking records, and all business communications sent via computer.

When we finally do have free time, our friends are all on social media sites and the only way to communicate with them was to join up, which in the end is a drug that infects your mind and pulls you further and further into the cyber world. Funding for public parks could someday stop altogether because no one would use them, opting instead for visiting cyber parks and building cyber farms. No, she didn't miss any of that at all. Assuming I get out of this alive, I'm not sure I want to go back to that life she thought.

Whether it was being on the ship or living in a time when such things as computers and cars didn't exist, her eyes and mind opened to new possibilities. She felt a great weight lifted off her, not having the chore of checking email to see if anyone had sent a message that demanded an immediate reply.

She felt the air moving in and out of her body as if it were the first breath she had ever taken. She heard sounds clearly and wondered if her hearing was indeed better here in this dimension. Her eyes traveled to the beam her hammock was swinging below. It was huge, easily twelve inches by twelve inches. Such a large beam would give strength, but also flexibility. The wood beam emitted warmth and gave the ship a feeling of life, its own life, separate and apart from the passengers.

The groaning of the composite of all the beams, as the ship cleaved through the water, became the voices of the trees that made this ship. Were they sad to be chopped down or happy to be sailing the seas, Emily wondered? Staring at the beam, her physical boundaries seemed to soften and with focus she could imagine herself becoming part of the ship, sailing with it as a partner rather than conquering it as a tool.

She understood now why true sailors preferred wooden ships to the sexy fiberglass ships, and why the niche market of wooden yachts was making a comeback. With a wooden ship, you set out together to explore, in fiberglass you are alone. If she got back from this dream she would design wooden ships, rather than the metal and steel she was working on now.

All day she noticed things, trivial things and big things, which had escaped her attention over the past days. The way the sails moved with the wind, working together to move the ship forward, and the way the deck seemed to smile when the scrubbing was done and the brass gleamed. Life embodied in wood, cloth, wind, and metal to create a vessel that carried an odd collection of human life toward a future that defied explanation.

Yet somehow the explanation wasn't needed. Just as she had expanded her perimeter to encompass the ship, she felt an expansion in time to envelope the concept of her great, great, great, great, great, great, great, great, great, great, great grandmother being her own age along with all the intervening grandmothers, all of them dead in her time, although she was getting fuzzy on just what her time was. Time was suddenly fluid, past, and present existed simultaneously, side-by-side, just slightly out of phase with one another. The ship somehow navigated those shifts and allowed all times to exist together and yet exist in one specific time.

The confined space of the ship reduced Emily's ability to walk great distances as she was accustomed to doing. Her main exercise was hiking and just walking around town. Climbing the ropes was strengthening her arms and balance, but her leg muscles felt tight, and walking with long strides was what she craved. The deck was small, but not so small that a purposeful stride couldn't be reached on the straight-away along the deck railings. She was on her third circuit; she had figured one hundred laps was about a mile and passing by a small alcove of barrels near the door to the Captain's quarters when Maggie stepped out of the shadows and put her finger to her lips to shush Emily's cry of surprise.

"Quiet, listen," she whispered and pointed to the wall behind them. The door to the room was cracked open enough to hear voices inside. Mary and Bedalia were talking. Emily breathed as quietly as she could; Mary's voice was shrill and tense, Bedalia's honey-smooth but with a new edge to it.

"Where do you go off to?" Mary demanded. "You can't just leave us out here in the middle of the sea."

"Leaving you here in the middle of de sea wouldn't serve any of us now, would it?" Bedalia responded, the warmth of last night was gone. Emily tried to focus on Bedalia to see if she could understand what the argument was about. Unexpectedly brilliant colors of anger and jealousy filled her mind and she suddenly understood that Bedalia was angry and jealous that Blackbeard had married Mary. She was angry that it was through this tiny, young, pale woman that she needed to work to free the man she had loved since their first passionate lovemaking. Emily gasped and looked wide-eyed at her mother. She had never successfully read someone's mind; although it was a popular game she and her girlfriends had played when she was younger. Maggie continued to hold her finger against her own pursed lips and Emily bit her lip to avoid saying anything aloud.

Emily and Maggie could hear Mary huff herself into one of the tufted seat chairs that the captain's quarters warranted.

"Blackbeard's treasure is for you to find, but there will be difficulties. I'm afraid you must trust me," the tea woman explained.

"We agreed; the treasure is mine. You have no purchase on it once found or do you forget our bargain?" Mary asked tensely.

"Indeed, that is still the agreement. I have no interest in the treasure itself." Some of the tension left Mary's voice.

"Well then, what do we do next?"

"You need to find the little island on the map. Your daughters can help. Only as a group will you decipher the hidden messages."

"Can't you just magic us there or something like that?"

"No, you must find the treasure yourself or it is meaningless." Bedalia turned to leave. Mary sighed, "I will bring it forward to the crew tonight."

Emily and Maggie scrambled away from the hiding spot just as Bedalia pushed open the door and left the Captain's Quarters. They immediately began talking quietly to each other as if they had just been walking casually by. They looked up at Bedalia as she passed and nodded in her direction.

Emily tried to reconcile the strange feeling of being inside Bedalia's head. "I don't know how I did it, but I was able to feel what Bedalia was thinking."

"Really? What did you feel?"

"Violent flashes of red, orange, and green. Bedalia is jealous of Mary and angry with her."

As Emily and Maggie descended the wooden stairs to the galley a warm, spicy scent drifted up to meet them. Emily was still feeling the anger of Bedalia. She had never been able to see into someone like that before; it was a gift she had only read about. I'm not sure I'd like that all the time, it's unnerving to be that close to someone.

All the women except Mary had already gathered around the table laughing and talking when Emily and Maggie arrived. Laughter and herbs are the keys to good cooking, Izzie often said, and she had found a kindred soul in Henry.

"Did you know that Henry here is a cook back in England?"

It was the first bit of information they had on Henry, and everyone had an "interesting" or an "oh really" to say. Henry waved it off and went back to cooking.

79

"I'm sure he's a very good cook and we'll try him out tomorrow, but tonight I wanted the meal to be made by us, collectively."

Dinner tonight was to be chicken cacciatore made from fresh birds, kept in cages stacked on deck. Izzie always received her meat already dead and dressed, so she turned to Ester, who had no other choices in the 1700's than to deal with live game. Ester calmly twisted their necks in one smooth clean move which took the chicken from life to dinner in an instant. With the familiarity of years of practice, she proceeded to pluck them clean until except for the attached head and feet they resembled the chickens Emily bought at the local grocer. Henry produced a small trunk filled with tins of spice, his stock in trade, which delighted Izzie and she began explaining how to use them all to an attentive Henry. From barrels filled with sand she pulled carrots and turnips, kept eatable and safe from rats by the sand.

Caroline had a bottle of tincture on the table from the ship's first aid kit. Carefully dabbing the tincture with cotton pads, she tended to various pokes, cuts and blisters the women were gaining daily as they learned the finer points of sailing their ship, yet another indication they were not dreaming.

Winnie, a seamstress by trade, organized a few of the women into a sewing squad. In addition to almost daily repairs to sails and ropes, the team was tackling the clothes the women wore. Each had been given a canvas pair of loose britches and a blousy white top. This utilitarian ensemble protected them against the sun to a certain extent but offered no individuality. Using the clothes each had been wearing when they boarded the ship the sewing team customized the woman's clothes. Gradually sashes and patches of colorful fabric adorned the women sailors, but would their fashion statements help them find the treasure or elude Hornigold?

"Where's Mary?" Caroline asked.

Henry snorted. "She wants her dinner in the Captain's Quarters tonight. I guess down below isn't good enough for her."

"Did she say that?" Izzie asked.

"No, but I can tell." He picked up a plate and began spooning food on it to take up to the Captain's Quarters. Emily and Maggie looked at each other with quizzical looks. Surely Mary was coming down here to share the map.

Finally, unable to sit still Emily rose, "I'm going to see what Mary is up to," she whispered to her mother.

CHAPTER TEN

EMILY

Emily watched as Mary unfolded the small map onto the desk in her cabin and stared at the crude drawing with the X marked on it.

Despite having briefly shown them the map and the story behind how she found it, the women had not had any time with the map itself. The air in the cabin was warm. None of the three windows across the back of the cabin were open. The still air made the space feel small, like a crowded old attic. Like the tea shop where the world had turned crazy.

Under the windows was a low bench with cushions covered in worn chintz. Emily tried to imagine the sea captain who owned this ship before Mary found it derelict in St. Thomas. He would have been stoic and true to his land-living wife, who had lovingly decorated the cabin with her favorite colors so he would remember her on his long voyages, to places she would never see, with scents she would never smell.

Finally, Mary looked up at Emily.

"I had hoped this map wouldn't be needed. Bedalia's magic is strong, and I really didn't expect we would have to do anything to find the treasure." Her fingers were busy turning the skeleton key like a rosary. "She's been there, after all, shouldn't be much to get us back."

Emily watched emotions play on Mary's face. Anger, frustration, pride. "A little work to find the treasure won't hurt us," she said. Mary stiffened.

"I was raised that a proper, well-bred woman didn't work." Grace heard impatience creep into Mary's voice. *Ah, now we're getting to the heart of it.*

"You found the tower, the map, and this ship, got her ready to sail, all that counts as work."

"True," Mary agreed, "my father would be horrified," and that thought seemed to delight her for she perked up and smiled, "and I've had fun, look my skin is even a bit brown from the sun!" She stretched her arms out to show Emily their light brown color.

"Everything is different from the life I lived in Bath, and I want more of it and for that, I need my husband's treasure. It could be so easy, but that wretched Bedalia woman won't just transport us to the island or even better still to wherever the treasure is hidden." She carefully folded the map back into its little square and put it in her pocket.

The conversation around the large wooden table in the galley quieted as Mary and Emily walked down the stairs. No one spoke. The only sounds were that of the water slapping the sides

84

of the ship and hammocks creaking as they swayed. Henry stood with the plate of food destined for her cabin in his hands and a surprised look on his face.

"Good evening." Emily could barely hear her whisper.

The assembled group murmured a polite "good evening" at their collective grandmother and fell silent again. Mary took a deep breath, looking around at the galley deck. Emily went and sat down next to Maggie, who gave her a questioning look.

"You've all done so well learning to sail this large ship. I'm enormously proud of you. I only hope this map is as good as I think it is. Otherwise, you'll think me a silly fool for dragging you all out here to the middle of nowhere to search for treasure."

Emily slid over on the bench to make room for Mary.

"Have a seat, Captain."

"Please call me Mary. Captain implies so much more than I truly know."

She sat down next to Emily and folded her hands in her lap, the paper concealed inside. Emily nudged her with her arm, "*the map*," she whispered.

Mary took a deep breath, and slowly, as if moving too quickly would tear the precious document, she opened the map and laid it on the table before them.

The map was small, measuring about the size of a large index card, the old-fashioned kind kids use in high school to write term paper notes, in the days before the internet and laptop computers. The creases were definite but not worn through. Emily realized that in her time this map would be upwards of three hundred years old, but now it was new.

The handwriting was strong and bold. Emily could tell it had been written with a quill pen because drops of black ink punctuated the ends of letters and one drop had landed in the middle of the page. Or at least she thought it was a random drop, this was a real treasure map, and the blot could be a clue. In the center of the map was an island, crudely drawn but clearly showing an hourglass shape with a long isthmus between the halves.

A simple compass rose with a small N at the north was in the lower right-hand corner. A line of small dots or circles to the east of the island seemed to indicate a reef or smaller islands. In the upper right-hand corner, was a picture of a skeleton holding a flask in one hand and a spear in the other. A large heart was at the point of the spear and what looked like drops of blood flew off the heart. The map acted as a magnet, drawing everyone's attention. They all leaned in to get a better look. Mary sat stiff and upright, watching as the women closed in on the map. There was excitement in their eyes; the lure of treasure beyond their wildest dreams had captured their collective imaginations.

Sophia, a fifth-grade teacher, broke the awkward silence.

"Mary, this is wonderful. Do you know where this island is?" Mary shook her head, her eyes on her hands in her lap.

"I thought Bedalia would take us there, but we must find it ourselves. We are a pawn in some game."

"All right," Sophia continued, assuming her school teacher's voice, "how about other maps that we could compare this to?" Mary nodded no, her head still hanging down.

"Well then," Sophia exclaimed cheerfully, "this shall truly be a great adventure – in the vein of Homer. We know only that there is a treasure and for now, that is enough!" Mary looked up in gratitude and smiled. "We may be in the vein of Homer, but I pray that we are not pursuing the treasure in vain." Giggles began to break out, eventually leading to laughter so infectious that soon tears ran down their cheeks.

After the laughter died down, Henry, who had characteristically been back in the shadows, wandered over to a barrel in the corner and pulled off the top. He returned minutes later with a long, rolled paper in his hands. All eyes were upon him as he approached the table. The women at the side of the table moved to the end allowing him to set the paper on the table and he unrolled a sea chart of the Caribbean. An audible intake of air rose from the group. Mary gasped.

"Henry! Where did you get this?" she exclaimed.

"I found it yesterday while exploring the boxes, crates, and barrels for food and utensils. Lord knows if it is useful, but it is a map."

The women gathered around the two pieces of paper. It was like working on a jigsaw puzzle with a large group of people. Blackbeard's map was a middle piece and they needed to find where it fits. Lanterns lit the table and the two maps seemed to

87

glow in the lamplight. The small map passed around the circle so many times that Mary grew fearful that it would tear. With so many eyes it didn't take long to find multiple sets of islands that matched.

It was long after midnight when the moon had risen and set, that they settled on one island with an isthmus in the middle and smaller islands to the east. The tiny island lay within a larger chain of islands and was protected from the ocean by reefs and barrier islands. They had a destination, they just needed to know where they were now. They didn't have to wait long before one of the women spoke up.

This time it was Madeline, a poised well-refined woman who other than her conversation with Emily on deck, had been quiet. She had been born in 1890 and had seen the century turn in grand style. Winnie, Madeline's mother, had given her up for adoption to an important family in the New England area. They had raised her as a proper, old money American girl and she had wed at seventeen to a man twice her age.

Initially excited about the idea of being a grown-up woman, she soon soured on the isolation and stigma of being wealthy. All their friends were wealthy too, and in Madeline's opinion, too concerned about the dresses and jewelry and not enough about the real world. The one highlight for her had been sailing. On the open ocean she had felt free, tasting the salty air, and letting the wind blow her otherwise coffered hair as it pleased.

"I know how to read the signs and figure out roughly where we are. My husband taught me…" her voice trailed off. Emily, who felt the freedom of having no husband, felt that Madeline had seen the act of her husband teaching her this skill as demeaning and that confessing to it was embarrassing.

"Maddie, that is wonderful!" Mary exclaimed. "It is so amazing that amongst us we seem to have everything we need,"

Madeline's eyes began to moisten with tears.

"Glad to help," was all she could get out without letting the muffled sob escape.

Choruses of "what's wrong" rang out.

"I've never been called by a nickname before, I've always been Madeline, and no one has cared enough to give me one…" she sobbed.

"Would you like us to call you Maddie?" Emily asked. Madeline looked up at her and nodded.

"Ok then, everyone, from now on Madeline Winchester Smythe will be known as Maddie. Got it?" Everyone nodded, smiling at Maddie.

"Ok then," Emily continued, "before Maddie goes off and figures out where in blue-blazes we are I'd like to know more about this…" and she pointed to the skeleton figure in the corner of the tower map.

Mary ran her finger over the skeleton. "I know about this." She sat quietly for a moment.

"Every pirate flies a Jolly Roger, that's what their flag is called, and this is Blackbeard's. I don't know what the flask means, maybe his love of rum, but the spear and the heart I can say for sure. He was a brute, and killed many, although fewer than stories tell. He used intimidation to scare his victims and they often surrendered without a fight, preferring to be stranded on islands rather than being killed, although that usually led to death anyway, I'm told." Henry cleared his throat.

"I'm sure the stories exaggerate Eddie's ways."

Mary's eyes were wide, as the imagined brutalities playing before her eyes mixed with the very real pain he had inflicted upon her.

"Why do you call him Eddie?" Winnie asked. Henry shrugged and drifted back into the darkness.

No one had noticed that Bedalia had joined them, so silently had she entered, and everyone jumped when she spoke.

"Flying Blackbeard's Jolly Roger will provide aid and support to you."

"Bedalia, you gave me a real start!" Mary placed her hand over her heart.

"You mean actually making this flag and flying it on this ship?" Caroline asked.

"Aye, I do."

"Pirates," Sophia said quietly to herself. Her tone was lost in thought but so full of dread that everyone stopped talking and stared at her. She looked up and exhaled a deep, worried sigh.

"I've studied them a bit you know…the man that killed Blackbeard went on to sail the Caribbean hunting other pirates. Lieutenant Maynard was his name, and he worked for the Governor of Virginia. He saw himself as a pirate killer unparalleled on the seas. There were rumors of others involved, including the Governor of the Bahamas and Massachusetts. They thought killing Blackbeard would intimidate all the other pirates to retreat and cease pirating.

Of course, that didn't work; it only made them madder in some cases, causing them to attack seaport towns just because they were there, for no other commercial gain. I never knew why I was so fascinated with pirates until now. Point is, we are not alone out here in the water, and flying a pirate flag puts us in league with them. Maynard may still be out here hunting pirates and if we fly that flag, we'll be hunted right along with them.

"Raise the flag," Bedalia repeated.

"I don't know," Caroline said shaking her head, "that seems creepy to me. I mean he's dead, seems like bad luck."

"Raising a pirate flag will mark us as pirates," Henry's voice came from the shadow. Maggie picked up the map and held it closer to the flame. Flickers of light danced on the paper.

"If flying the flag of Blackbeard affords us any protection at all, then I say fly it. Hopefully his ghost will help us, and we're going to need all the help we can get. I say we take Bedalia's suggestion."

Bedalia fixed Mary with a stare.

91

"Blackbeard - he needs to be free of his treasure, he'll help you."

Using the ships charts, clock, sextant and the stars, Maddie quickly determined their position to be 23° 14" and the needed course to be southwest. Bedalia directed them in setting the sails so that the ship was heading into a southern vector and according to the map the islands of interest were sitting at around 15 °.

"I estimate with a good trade wind we should reach 15 ° in 3 days." Emily took down all the information and recorded it in the ship's log.

"We need rotational shifts to keep us on course and moving twenty-four hours a day. I suggest four-hour shifts, two of us at a time."

Mary raised her hand. "Emily, I'll join you for the first shift." They left for the wheel deck to assume their first watch. First and last, alpha and omega, bound for treasure. Would flying the flag of a hated pirate be a blessing or a curse?

First, they had to make a flag though, and making a flag seemed to put them one step closer to being pirates themselves.

CHAPTER ELEVEN

EMILY

Palpable excitement rippled through the women as they settled into the ship's routine of swabbing the decks, mending the sails, and ensuring general good order. In just a few days the decrepit ship was now gleaming, varnish having been scraped and reapplied, brass polished, rotten wood replaced, and ropes were rewoven and neatly coiled. Even the sails were patched. With only fifteen people on board, they were always busy. Ever shifting teams of women working day and night knit together a family narrative as strong as the sails and ship they were repairing. Bedalia had disappeared again, which provided the main fodder for the evening meal discussion. Henry became more of an active crew member, but even he couldn't explain Bedalia.

On the eighth day, Emily awoke to a steady drumming sound. She swayed in her hammock listening to the beat as she slowly moved through the fog in her head. It was raining, a slow steady rain. Water dripped from the ceiling and Emily made note of where they needed to patch the deck above to block the water. She lingered in her hammock, knowing that chores outside would be delayed, and she could stay in that luxurious state of being almost, but not quite, asleep. Her thoughts drifted to the baby growing in her belly. Would this baby be born?

'I'm either dead and this is heaven, I'm dreaming in which case I'll wake up, or this is real, in which case I have no good explanation, whatever the facts, I have some amazing ancestors and belong to a proud family of strong women.

Emily herself was feeling more self-confident. It felt like she had come out from under gauze which blurred the colors of the world. As a descendent of Blackbeard, the Pirate, she had warrior sailing genes flowing through her, expressing for the first time. The child she carried would have the same lineage, the same yearning for the sea. Emily wanted to know this child, to watch her grow into her full potential and carry on the traditions, new traditions that were being formed daily on the ship by the women in her family.

The whistle of the teapot eventually vanquished the fog and she rolled out gracefully from her hammock and shuffled over towards the galley. Not many were up, taking advantage of this unexpected reprieve; they chose to remain cocooned in sleep. Henry alone was working in the galley and handed her a cup of the hot brew as she sat down at the wooden table.

"Beautiful day, isn't it?"

"I suppose so," Emily said, sipping the steaming tea, wondering if this was the same tea that she had before walking out the tea shop door onto the deck of *The Maryann*.

"I've got all the empty barrels up top to catch the rain. Fresh water isn't easy to come by on the sea you know." He turned to poke the coals of the stove.

"I hadn't thought about it, but I see your point. I can wash my hair."

"It also makes us harder to track," Henry said. He put a bowl of porridge in front of Emily.

"What do you mean harder to track? Who's tracking us?" A knot of fear settled in her chest.

"Remember Bedalia told you about Hornigold? He was with Ed and her on the little island. He wants the treasure too and has been waiting for someone to go after it. He's a lazy cur and will let others do the work for him. He'll be lying in wait for us and will follow us to the treasure. We need to be ready for him, I'm sure he will attack once you have the treasure."

Emily put her spoon down. Being pursued by some treasure-hungry pirate wasn't something they had figured into their plans.

"How do we avoid him?"

"That will be hard, he is an expert sailor, and his ship is smaller and faster. Learn to use the sword well; I fear you will need it before we're done."

"Uh, yea," was all Emily could say, dread filling her heart.

95

"I think I'll go on deck and enjoy the rain." She climbed the stairs to the steady drumming sound of water hitting the wooden deck. This journey sounded more dangerous every day and becoming more pirate-like seemed to be the key to survival.

CHAPTER TWELVE

EMILY

Sitting watch in the crow's nest at the top of the mainmast was a coveted job, as it was one of the few places on the ship where you could be alone with your thoughts. Despite the inclement weather, or maybe because of it, high above their heads, Emily could see that Ann, Mary's daughter, was on duty. The rain slowed to a stop as the ship sailed out from under the storm clouds. Ann shook the tarp that covered her, sending more water raining down on the deck.

Notwithstanding Mary's contribution to the family history, Ann was really the start of the story. Born in 1719, just eleven months after the date of the journey they were on, Ann had grown to young adulthood in an adopted home in the same town as her mother, but did not know that one fact, until now. Ann had shared with Emily that she had heard the stories about Blackbeard and Mary, but never noticed the strong resemblance she had to the young woman known as the Widow Teach. Mary had gone to the

Caribbean when Ann was a baby and returned when she was two. The presence of one more girl child was of no consequence. Ann herself had never made the connection, despite wagging tongues and sideward glances.

Ann's alert in her clear voice drifted down to the deck, "Ship's sails to the starboard bow!"

Everyone still asleep tumbled out of their hammocks and ran up the stairs to the top deck, starboard side, and strained their eyes to see the other ship. Ann, with her vantage over sixty feet in the air, could see beyond the horizon, and it took a few minutes for Emily to see the ship's sails.

Emily turned to Mary and asked, "Do we have a pair of binoculars?" Mary simply looked at Emily with a question in the brows of her eyes.

"What is a binocular?"

"Shoot, that's right, they haven't been invented yet. How about a…." Emily struggled to think what it might have been called, "a seeing glass that makes distant things look close," resorting to describing the thing she couldn't name.

"Ah yes, you mean a spyglass," Mary turned to fetch the object from the Captain's Quarters. She returned holding a brass, segmented spyglass and handed it to Emily who took the glass, adjusted the eyepiece, and located the ship.

"I see it, wow this isn't as easy as it looks, with the ship's rocking on the water and wind blowing my arm it's hard to keep it steady." Mary watched as Emily peered through the spyglass. Henry came limping up beside them.

"It's flying a flag of some sort, I can barely see it," Emily reported. By now a knot of women had gathered around her, along with Bedalia, who had mysteriously appeared again, with Ann's call of warning. Bedalia took the glass from Emily and peered through it.

"Hornigold." Her voice dripped with disgust. Henry took the glass from Bedalia and stared hard at the flag.

"Sure is."

"Who's Hornigold? I remember you mentioned him but who exactly is he?" Winnie asked.

"A pirate gone bad," Bedalia took the glass back and examined the distant ship.

"How can a pirate go bad?" Maddie asked from the outer rim of the circle, "I thought they were already bad."

Bedalia handed the glass to Mary.

"Aye, you could say that. But amongst the pirating world, there is a code, the Code of the Brethren, and pirates live by it, and die by it... Hornigold is a pirate that broke the code and now hunts down and kills pirates when he's not pirating himself." She spat on the floor as if spitting on the pirate hunter. Horrified looks followed the spittle down to the well-scrubbed deck.

"Well, we aren't pirates, so we have nothing to worry about, right?" Mary nodded her head as if that would make the answer yes.

"Aye and nay," Henry answered. "He won't be hunting us to kill us, but he will be wanting the treasure."

"How does he know about the treasure?" Ann asked.

"He may have heard about Mary and figured that she has the map and knows where the treasure is. He'll be following us just to be sure, and if needs be, I'm sure he'll step in after we've found it, to take it."

"Well then," Mary asked calmly, "how do we evade him?" Emily didn't think evading him was possible. She could see that Hornigold's sloop was gaining on them, clearly a faster ship with sailors who knew what they were doing.

The Maryann was wide and flat, stable but slow, and outrunning them seemed unlikely. There were no other islands in sight yet, and if the estimate of their current location was correct, then they had one more day of open sea before approaching a chain of islands that could hide them. They were sitting ducks. If Bedalia was right, then Hornigold wouldn't want to overtake them, but merely shadow them until they had led him to the treasure.

That was small comfort as Emily was now sure that when Hornigold grew weary of the chase, he might board and take the map and then locate the treasure himself. Emily's heart was pounding in her chest as she realized that they were being hunted as surely as she and *The Maryann* were hunting the treasure. The family Mary founded was in jeopardy.

No one could think of an alternate course of action so they kept sailing on hoping that an idea would strike someone, but nothing did. As the day wore on the crew grew testy with each other, their nerves were taught and even the simplest of transgressions resulted in a snapped response. It was clear that Hornigold's ship could overtake them, but it didn't. It appeared Bedalia was right, Hornigold didn't want to capture them, and he wanted them to lead him directly to the treasure, where he would take it from them. His ship remained within sight and silently stalked *The Maryann.*

Also, on the horizon now were four more ships, caravanned behind Hornigold's. It looked like a slow boat parade with *The Maryann* in the front, Hornigold in the middle, and the four mystery ships sailing side by side bringing up the rear. The ponderous, flat-bottomed Maryann was no match for five ships and even Hornigold seemed to be rattled by the presence of the four ships. His speed became erratic as he alternately slowed to get a better look at his pursuers and sped up to close the distance between his sloop and *The Maryann,* yet every time Emily checked their progress in relation to the sloop it was closer. She could clearly see the flag now, a skull with two crossed bones under it and a star on top of the skull. Bedalia looked through the looking glass again and re-affirmed that it was Hornigold's flag.

"Remember, I sailed the seas a bit in my time, before that night on the island," she explained, "and that flag is burned into my memory."

Emily couldn't concentrate so she walked around the small center deck to burn-off energy.

101

"Aren't you getting dizzy?" Isabel asked after Emily had passed her for the third time.

"Yes, a little bit," Emily said, though she wasn't sure whether her queasy stomach was because of the baby or the circles.

"May I ask you a question?" she asked Isabel.

"Certainly."

"How did you know you were in love?"

"Whoever said I was in love?"

"Well, I just assumed you've fallen in love."

"Ha! It's a waste of time! The world doesn't didn't care that I loved a boy, it had no bearing on my future, and you must learn to accept the situation you are in, but love? It is not for me."

Her statement was so adamant that Emily was left wondering what had happened to her great grandmother, but one thing she was sure of was that Isabel had loved, yet something had turned her against it. Emily turned to the rail and leaned against it.

"I've met a guy who might be the one." Mark's face seemed to hover over the water in front of her. His blond hair was blowing in the sea breezes and his blue eyes held the same degree of concern she saw when she told him she was pregnant.

"I'm trying to figure it out."

"I can't give you any advice on knowing whether you are in love, but I can give you some general advice. Hide everything of value you have and don't let him know where it is, or he will take it and sell it."

Her eyes looked teary. Emily realized Isabel had loved, but her love had not protected her or valued her. She nodded her head at her distant relative and went back to staring at the water.

The crew sailed earnestly the remainder of the day, yet desperation began to settle in as the sun began to set. If all had gone according to plan, they would awake the next morning to a chain of islands that contained the little hourglass-shaped island. As it was, Hornigold would be on top of them at the pace he was making and there would be no way to stop him from finding the location of the island.

The four mystery ships would also find the island and their intentions were not as clear as Hornigold's. As the sun reached the horizon, the four ships behind Hornigold's sloop were painted gold. They were close enough for Emily to see clearly through the spyglass, they looked much bigger than *The Maryann* or the sloop. The flags they were flying looked official, not like a pirate standard. Who were they and who were they interested in, *The Maryann* or Hornigold? Was *The Maryann* leading a parade to the treasure and if so, would they get out of this with their treasure or their lives?

CHAPTER THIRTEEN

EMILY

Emily and Maggie had the watch together that night. They had become a pair, doing things together without noticing it. Mother and daughter. Emily found Maggie a good partner for the sailing tasks and enjoyed the discussions they had while working. Philosophy, religion, music, and the odd situation they found themselves in were favorite topics, everything but Emily's pregnancy. Maggie seemed to respect the silence Emily kept about the baby. She didn't ask whether Emily intended to keep it or the circumstances around how she got pregnant. It wasn't that Emily didn't think about the baby, on the contrary, it occupied a lot of her thoughts. She feared it was fanciful thinking though. Emily went over and over her conversation with Mark, looking for clues in his words and reactions. He would support her, but what did that mean? Would he drive her to the abortion clinic or stand by her and the child for the next twenty or thirty years?

"You know," Maggie said that night, "if it weren't for being chased by a real pirate and whoever those other guys are, this is about as perfect a vacation as you can imagine." Emily laughed. It was true; warm weather, fresh air, good exercise, and a chance to live like a pirate were great fun. The treasure hunt was exhilarating and while not standard vacation fare, meeting your long dead relatives and the mother you only dreamt about was amazing.

"How true. Assuming we return to our lives before this weirdness, it will be a boring existence. And the salt air is doing wonders for my dreams." She held the wheel steady, instinctively maintaining course, and relayed her latest dream. After the first few days where Emily fell quickly into a dead sleep that contained no dreams, last night the vivid sailing dreams had resumed, with the added dimension that now a pirate was part of the dreams. She assumed it was Blackbeard, which only made sense because she was his descendent. Last night's dream had been of the hour-glass shaped island. She saw a cave, halfway up the mountain at the isthmus of the island, hidden by a large thicket of bushes. Its entrance was guarded by a shrunken head hanging from the top of the arch that formed the doorway. It was a hideous thing, no doubt not happy to be hanging alone on an island, separate from the rest of its body, which was nowhere to be found in her dream. The head blocked the path somehow, and kept asking for a password, but Emily didn't know the password and couldn't enter the cave.

"Sounds very Hollywood, are you sure you're a boring engineer?" Maggie smiled. In the moonlight, Emily watched the wind pick up a locket of her mother's hair and toss it to the wrong side. Maggie lifted her hand to pat it back into place when all her hair stood up straight. Emily laughed and then noticed that hers was doing the same thing. The laugh caught in Emily's throat as she noticed the dark funnel cloud over Maggie's shoulder. Visible even in the darkness, it swirled ferociously, reaching from the highest clouds to the sea itself.

Years of having lived near the sea told her this was a water spout and a large one at that. She pointed to it and shouted, "storm!" Maggie whirled and saw it spiraling into the sky. At its feet a maelstrom was forming, the sea swirling down to the center of the earth. Emily screamed and raced to get Bedalia, she was convinced the woman would know what to do, with Maggie right behind her. She thought briefly of tying the wheel to the railing, to try to keep the rudder straight, but the size of the storm made that unnecessary. That small act of control would only constrain the ship, and like a horse in a storm, it needed its head to survive.

When Emily arrived below deck, Bedalia and Henry had already roused the crew and they were all busy lashing things down with ropes that Henry was pulling out of barrels. The lanterns were swaying from side to side, causing wildly leaping light and shadows. The last ropes he pulled from the barrels he began handing to the women. Finally, Bedalia doused the flame in the galley's cast iron stove and securely shut the door on the still-hot coals.

"Everyone up on deck and tie one end of the rope to your waist and another to something that won't blow overboard," Bedalia shouted above the increasing wind. Maggie grabbed two ropes from Henry in one hand, reached out and snagged Emily's hand in the other, and began dragging her back up to the deck. She had lost her daughter once and she was determined to not let that happen again.

"Henry needs help with the stairs," Emily called out as Maggie pulled her up the wood stairs. Maggie didn't slow down and didn't show any sign she had heard Emily and reluctantly Emily let herself be pulled up to the deck.

The seas were heaving now, and walking was becoming difficult. The sky was black, loose barrels were rolling around, and the sails were straining to contain the wind. Quickly, Maggie led Emily to the main mast and began lashing the ropes to the mast and around their waists. That done she picked up a rope laying on the deck and tying the two of them together, made another loop around the great mast.

Emily stared out at the dark sky and foaming seas. Hornigold's ship, barely visible in the darkness was bobbing up and down in the water, yet still managing to be gaining on them. Past Hornigold, just at the edge of the moving horizon Emily could see the four mystery ships, appearing and disappearing with the waves. Their sails glowed white, despite the storm, as if lit by something else entirely. Mary was tied to the railing, holding onto the slippery wood with white knuckles. Henry had made it to the deck and was tying himself to the side railing next to Mary.

The Maryann lurched toward the maelstrom with Hornigold's ship close behind. Emily could see Hornigold now, a large man in a blue frock coat with gold trim. His hat was festooned with a large peacock feather, the overall look being that of a pompous gentleman of leisure. He was watching *The Maryann* through his spyglass and seemed to be locked onto the sight of Mary. His crew jumped at an order he barked and within seconds the sloop pulled up next to *The Maryann* and a grappling hook flew, anchoring the two ships together. It happened so fast the lumbering Maryann didn't have a chance of moving out of the way.

"Mary, watch out!" Emily and Maggie called out together, but it was too late. In a practiced move, Hornigold leaped to the deck of *The Maryann*, slashed the rope Mary had used to tie herself to the railing, picked her up like a toy, and swung back to the sloop. A sailor ran up and sliced the grappling hook rope and the two ships parted, the heavier Maryann beginning to slide down into the whirlpool ahead of the sloop. Henry stood slack-jawed at the brazen act he had just seen and done nothing to stop.

"They've got Mary, Bedalia, what do we do?" Emily screamed. Her voice couldn't be heard over the sound of the storm, and if a response were given, it was lost too. Emily could see the sloop and the four other ships dip into the whirlpool swirling in ever tighter circles, making Emily dizzy and nauseous.

She thought of the baby, thought about Mark and her mother Maggie. She tried to keep herself focused, but it was too much, and darkness slipped over her. Whatever was going to happen was going to happen without her knowing it.

CHAPTER FOURTEEN

MARY

Mary stood lashed to the railing of the wrong ship. The knot she had tied herself to the railing of *The Maryann* with had gotten wet and too hard to untie as Hornigold's sloop closed the distance between the two ships. She had been unable to flee the attack and now found herself a captive aboard an enemy ship. The pirates ignored her, after ensuring she was tied securely to their ship's railing because the sloop was sliding into the whirlpool after *The Maryann*. It really didn't matter which ship she was tied to, both ships seemed doomed to certain death.

Mary wracked her memory for a story of a ship having escaped such a storm, but nothing came to mind, a maelstrom was a storm to be feared for a reason. Ships were inhaled by the sea, never to be seen again.

"Man, the canvas, keep them tight," Hornigold called out over the growing din of wind. He was so preoccupied with the hole that had opened in the sea that he nearly missed seeing the water spout climbing up into the sky as if all the water missing from the hole was being thrown up into the air.

The sloop had sailed thirty feet down into the turning, inverted twister when Hornigold saw the four ships slip over the edge one by one; the edge of the maelstrom hole was widening to capture them. The six ships slowly circled in the funnel, sailing skills useless at this point, gravity, nature, and luck were all that mattered.

The larger military ships, less maneuverable and much heavier were drawn down faster. In two turns of the watery spiral, the four military ships were one hundred feet lower down; Hornigold had somehow managed to maintain his position at thirty feet, right behind *The Maryann*, which despite its weight was holding steady at forty feet. Around and around the ships circled, a dull feeling of gravity and centrifugal force pushing Mary to the deck. She lost sight of *The Maryann* at that moment and felt isolation wash over her like the waves of seawater starting to slosh onto the deck from the sides of the maelstrom.

At the point where it felt the ship would careen sideways into the bottomless hole, Mary watched as the water spout moved past Hornigold's ship quickly and converged with the center of the maelstrom, each working against the other and each beginning to cancel out the other. As the water spout lowered down, the water level rose, pushing the sloop up and out of the hole and onto the churning surface.

"Hard to port!" Hornigold called out when they were free of the death spiral and the ship careened left, making slow progress in the still unstable air. Mary hung onto the railing where she was tied, watching as the expansive water spout finished settling back into the sea. Minutes went by and not so much as a piece of wood or sail cloth floated by.

Mary looked around frantically for *The Maryann*. It was gone, completely gone, as were the four larger ships that had been chasing Hornigold. The sea had swallowed *The Maryann* and the four warships completely and Mary, Hornigold, and his men had gotten out with their lives. The water was calming, the sky clearing to blue, the wind fair and breezy, and no Maryann. Her newly found family, daughter, and granddaughters were nowhere to be seen. As quickly as the storm started, it ended with a devastating result. Mary had survived the storm and *The Maryann* and her crew had not.

Two of the sails had torn in the storm and the crew quickly began adjusting the ropes to compensate. Water drained off the deck over the sides and despite some residual choppy water, some level of normalcy settled over the ship. Sailors were crossing themselves in the style of the Catholic Church at having survived certain death. Mary, drenched to the bone and still tied to the railing, could only despair at having lost so much so quickly. Where was Bedalia and why had she not protected them all from this?

Hornigold calmly walked over to Mary swinging a large blade and with a swift swipe cut the ropes tying her to the railing.

"Ye won't be going anywhere now, milady, Captain Hornigold at your service," he bowed then roughly grabbed her wrist and led her across the deck into the Captain's Quarters through ornately decorated glass doors. The toothless grins of the pirates made Mary's flesh crawl. What was Hornigold going to do with or to her? Once in the Captain's quarters he closed the door.

"I know you have the map."

"I don't know what you are talking about…And if I did have a map, it is lost to the storm now."

"Come, come, my dear. I have reliable sources that tell me that you spent days in that wretched tower in Charlotte Amalie, then suddenly bought a ship and sailed away. You must have found the map."

Mary needed time to think. Her eyes roamed around the small captain's quarters, much smaller than her own aboard *The Maryann*, but richly appointed with a variety of woods. In the center was a large table covered with maps, a bunk was tucked into the side and a long, cushioned window seat ran along the back under a huge window.

"What if I did? I don't have it on me; your kidnapping was in vain."

"Perhaps," Hornigold walked over to his map table. "but you've seen it, you no doubt remember enough to point me in the right direction."

Mary could see the logic of his assumption and struggled to think of a way to distract him.

"I'm just a young girl, captain, with an empty head. I rely totally on my crew to sail the ship and follow any silly maps." She hoped it sounded true enough. Then she went on the offensive.

"What happened to the ships who were trailing you? We saw them through the spy glass."

"Hopefully swallowed by the sea, just as your ship has been. Look around, you won't see it. You have me to thank for your life, and my reward is the treasure."

"I don't believe you. I want to see for myself that they are indeed gone."

"I am not a fool; you will stay here with me Mrs. Teach."

"Who were the men in those ships?" she asked, still trying to distract him from the map. Hornigold walked over to the back window and twirled his mustache with his fingers.

"I've wondered that myself. They were big ships, extremely fast. I suspect they are from the Virginia Navy and that can mean only one thing – that menace Lieutenant Maynard is hunting me. The scallywag who killed Blackbeard, your husband, is hunting me, hunting me as a pirate with the intent of killing me."

"Peter!" Hornigold called out to his first mate and a wiry-looking fellow popped his head into the room.

"Make sure we are flying my flag, the flag that gives me the authority of the Governor of the Bahamas, Governor Rogers, to sail in these waters and hunt pirates myself."

"Aye captain, she's flying as high as we can get her," Peter replied. Hornigold waved his hand at him and Peter retreated from the room, quietly closing the door behind him.

"This is most disturbing. The only way Maynard could know where to find me, and ignore my flag, is if Rogers told him and that means Woodes Rogers, the Governor of the Bahamas Islands is trying to eliminate me, to betray me to the eager lieutenant. Doesn't he know we are on the same side?" Hornigold asked Mary. Mary nodded her head in agreement. Always agree with men who are rambling, her mother had taught her, it is the safest course of action.

"I'm a legitimate business man," Hornigold was talking to himself now, Mary having been forgotten. "When the king's pardon arrived, I was first in line. I have a large plantation and my own ships. I've helped rid the seas of dangerous pirates. My neck should be safe." Hornigold seemed lost in thought when he suddenly turned towards Mary.

"I met Edward Teach as a young seafarer originally from Bristol, eager to prove his mettle. He was a big, ambitious, educated kid, a diamond in the rough. It was easy to give him a pirating name, his thick black beard hung fully from his face, and in battle he lit oil lamp wicks or bomb fuses and tucked them into his beard to create a halo of smoke. It was a remarkable sight! It frightened more than a few into surrender. He had a sailor's appetite for wine, women and of course violence. I promoted him quickly, giving him his own ship to captain, which he promptly named the Queen Anne's Revenge. We sailed together for a brief time and parted ways as friends. At least I thought we were. The incident on the island may have changed that."

"What incident?" Mary asked, sure it was the same one Bedalia had shared.

"It was on a little island somewhere south west of Tortuga. We were looking for the island where Captain Morgan buried his treasure and heard talk that the island, we were on was it, but we couldn't find it. We hunted for weeks, drank rum and hunted for treasure. It was just Ed, Bedalia and me. Bedalia was one of the best pirates I ever sailed with. I loved her, but she didn't love me, she loved only Ed. When we couldn't find the treasure, we drank and the drinking led to a fight," his voice trailed off. "Somehow in the fight, shots were fired, and Bedalia was hit. Ed and I were too drunk to notice, and it wasn't till morning that we found her, bled to death on the beach."

Stiffly Hornigold stood straight and pulled down on the Commander's coat he wore. "Ed drew a map so we would remember the island's locations. I think you found it in the tower and I want you to describe to me."

"If you've been there before you shouldn't need a map, simply retrace your steps. That always works for me when I've lost something," Mary prattled on, hoping she sounded sufficiently empty headed so as not to warrant Hornigold's time.

"If it were that easy, don't you think I would have taken the treasure before this?" he exploded. "No, Blackbeard was sneaky and sailed me around drunk for days. I have no idea where I was or where the island is. I've searched every map there is and can't find anything that looks familiar. You are my key to finding the treasure. I advise you to cooperate or the consequences could be very dire for you. You may join the crew of your ship in the briny deep."

CHAPTER FIFTEEN

EMILY

Maggie shouted over the roaring wind "Hold on! Shut your eyes and hold on. I lo..." Her last words were blown away by the storm which hit the ship square on with a ferocity Emily had never imagined possible.

She closed her eyes tightly and squeezed her hands on the ropes, holding on with every ounce of strength she had. Screams from the other women blew by and she prayed that they had all secured themselves in time. The storm roared like a train in her ears, and even if she had wanted to open her eyes, the force of the wind kept them shut. She could feel a pull on the ropes tied around her waist and knew that she was lashed to not only the great mast but to her mother, Maggie.

Try as she might, she couldn't get her hands to slide along the rope to see if she could touch Maggie's hands. They were inches apart, but that distance seemed immeasurable. Years of getting dizzy on even the slowest merry-go-round told her that the ship was moving in a slow, big circle. Were they in the storm above the water or in the great maelstrom driving down to the sea bottom?

Emily struggled to open her eyes, even a tiny slit, to see what was happening, and was able to open them but just barely. The ship was contained in a whirling column; nothing was visible past the ship except the wall of wind circling up. The force of the wind was less now because the ship was moving with it and she found she could open her eyes fully.

Around her she saw the crew tied to various objects; railings, the wheel, banisters, and everyone was now standing and looking at the tube of wind in which they were now encased. Emily felt the characteristic cold sweat of nausea building on her upper lip. How high would the ship go, she wondered.

Time stood still and how long they were in the storm no one would be able to tell later. The only clock on board fell over and broke in the wind, its hands moved by the force of the fall. Hours, minutes, or seconds passed, hard to tell really. Gradually the sound of the storm amplified, and the wind picked up again and Emily's eyes were forced shut. The ship set down on the ocean again and rocked wildly as the storm fizzled out and vanished as quickly as it came up.

Emily carefully opened her eyes and saw sunshine and placid water, as if the great storm had never occurred. The crew began untying and looking around to make sure everyone was okay. As soon as Maggie untied them Emily scaled the nearest ropes to reach the crow's nest, her legs moving effortlessly.

"I see an island," she called down, "and we're alone, no sign of the sloop, or Mary."

Miraculously, no one was seriously hurt in the storm. Everyone had scratches or bruises from the ropes or flying debris, but considering the scale of the storm, and the disappearance of Hornigold's ship and whoever else had been approaching, they all agreed that something had protected them.

"I told you flying Ed's Jolly Roger would protect you," Bedalia smiled. Ever since seeing the flag of Blackbeard on the map, the crew had been recreating it. The availability of black cloth was limited so it was more colorful than the black and white of the original.

"But we haven't raised the flag yet, it's not done," Caroline said.

"Well best you do that straight away then for the magic will be stronger."

"I still don't understand how he could be helping us," Winnie said.

"I can't contact him until he is freed of the treasure, but I trust he will help you, and trust is a strong bond."

"Maybe he is looking to redeem himself," Elaine said. She had been born in 1805, after the age of the Atlantic pirates was finally over. Her professional writings of romantic love and poems of epic journeys were flavored by the colorful stories still carried occasionally in the papers about the pirates.

"I read about pirates and many repented later in life. Perhaps Blackbeard died too soon and didn't have time to repent." Emily couldn't see a pirate with the reputation of Blackbeard making a clean go of it.

"I doubt he would have repented later. But I could see that in death the better side of him might come out. In any event, we are out of the storm; Hornigold seems to have vanished, taking Mary with him. How on earth do we find Mary? We can't just go on without her."

"I agree," Ann said, "We can't go on without Mary, she's why we are all here."

"Ann and Mary are the only ones who live in this time. Bedalia, what happens now?" Emily asked.

Bedalia looked at them with her steady gaze. "We go on. They won't hurt Mary; they think she will lead them to the treasure."

"But we can't know that for certain," Ann said, "can we?"

Convinced as they were that the islands in front of them were the very islands they were looking for, out came the map again and heads bowed over it to identify shoals, reefs, and anything else that could impede their way.

Every woman who had duty before the wheel over the next twelve hours studied and memorized the path until it was committed to permanent memory. The little hour glass shaped island proved easy to find and by the end of the day the ship sat at anchor in the isthmus.

They had found the island but had lost Mary. Was the treasure going to be worth the price?

CHAPTER SIXTEEN

MARY

Hornigold led Mary to the map table.

"Show me the island." His voice demanded and left no room for negotiation. Mary studied the map carefully, looking for an hour-glass shaped island as far away from the one she had been headed for. After a long search, she found one, off the coast of Jamaica. She pointed to it. "There it is. That's the island we were headed for. I'm not sure where we are now, but that is our destination."

Hornigold put his finger on the island "We are as far away from that as you can get in these waters. Are you sure?"

Mary lowered her eyes and tried to look demure.

"We are not good sailors, so I'm not surprised that we were on the wrong side of the sea. Of course, it doesn't matter now; my ship and crew are gone. Will you be taking me back to the Bahamas?"

"Ah, my good lady, I won't be taking you anywhere. At least anywhere you want to go. I will be leaving you on the nearest island, where I assume you will oblige me by dying and taking my quest to your grave."

Mary gasped. She wasn't sure whether he had accepted her story of the location of the map, but it appeared he had. Being released onto an island to fend for yourself was a common fate of those captured by pirates. It was effective because food and water were a scarce resource, and many poisonous plants covered the islands, assuming there were any plants at all. Hungry and thirsty, the hapless survivor would eat something that would cause hallucinations, convulsions and eventually death.

"Please sir!" I've told you where the island is. You have your heading. I will stay quietly below decks and not bother your crew. Let me stay on board until you reach the Bahamas," she pleaded.

Hornigold laughed at the obvious fright in her voice.

"Nay, Peter!" he yelled. Peter appeared almost immediately at the door again. He must just stand out there waiting for Hornigold to call, Mary thought.

"Take us to the nearest island," he commanded.

"Aye sir, nearest island," Peter repeated, "we're near a small island now sir."

"That will do. I want to get this woman off my ship as soon as possible, she's bad luck." He smiled one of the nastiest smiles Mary had ever seen.

"And take this prisoner onto the top deck and tie her to the railing again, so she can survey the horizon and confirm for herself that her ship is truly gone."

Peter nodded and graciously held the door open for her. Mary stomped out of the Captain's Quarters showing as much indignity as she could and allowed herself to be led to the top deck and re-tied to the railing. At least she could breathe fresh air, and should *The Maryann* re-appear, have a chance at seeing it. By nightfall, the ship was anchored off a little island. She could see it was a green island, with a tall mountainous peak in the center. Mary remained tied to the railing, weakening from lack of food and water. The captain and his crew were uproariously drunk and had forgotten all about her.

Quietly she began to work the knot until it started to loosen. Looking around she saw where the anchor rope angled down into the water. She completed untying herself and slowly crept over to where the rope met the railing. A loud round of laughter drifted out of the captain's quarters and using that as cover she quickly scaled the railing and slid down the rope. Her hands burned as she slid, and the water came much faster than she expected.

The cool water on her hands felt good and she hoped that the splash wasn't audible inside the crowded cabin. Mary had never swum in the night before, and her heart pounded as she moved through the dark water.

Fortunately, she didn't have far to swim before her feet felt sand beneath her and soon she was walking along the water line looking for a suitable place to hide. The gentle surf on the beach would soon wash away her footprints. She didn't know how long it would be before they realized she was gone, and she wanted to put some distance between her and the ship. Stories of poisonous snakes and cannibals ran through her mind, but survival was her priority, so she pushed into the thick growth and disappeared into the island.

She didn't see Hornigold watching her from the railing, smiling as he watched her disappear into the deep jungle. She had saved him the effort of marooning her, and he had directions to the treasure.

CHAPTER SEVENTEEN

EMILY

Emily almost couldn't remember when she had last seen solid land, and the sight of it filled her heart with happiness. She leaned on the railing and watched the dry, unmoving land.

By her rough calculations, they had been on the ship for six or seven days but given all that had happened, she frankly didn't trust her own estimate. The ship was anchored about twenty yards from shore. The women were scrambling over the sides of the ship and swimming to shore, anxious to touch the beach. Maddie was in the lead with the strongest swim stroke, and she made the beach first, leaping on the hot sand and whooping loudly.

Dinner tonight would be onshore, and Henry, Bedalia, and Isadora came on deck carrying the spice box piled on top of a second box full of cooking utensils. They headed for the dinghy and after lowering the little rowboat into the water, tied ropes around the boxes and lowered them into the craft. Emily watched from the railing as the ship emptied. Maddie was still running around on the sand and diving in and out of the small waves breaking on the beach. She couldn't explain her own reluctance to descend the ropes and swim to shore herself.

"Quite a sight, isn't it?" Maggie came up beside Emily and leaned on the railing to look over. Emily nodded; looking at the mother she had sought and now wasn't quite sure how to talk to. Words tumbled in her brain, but nothing formed a coherent sentence. Maggie sensed her hesitation.

"I've been meaning to talk with you, but there just hasn't been a quiet moment or the right quiet moment. We've talked about a lot of things except the main things you are probably curious about." Emily had been planning, dreaming about, and dreading this moment ever since figuring out the history of the crew and realizing the mother whom she had wanted to meet more than anything was right here. Now that the answers were within reach, anger and curiosity broiled equally within Emily. Yes, it was true that all these women had been abandoned and all had remorse. But this particular woman had abandoned her. Left her with strangers and never came back to see how she was doing, to see what she looked like, experienced any of her childhood highs and lows.

"Who was my father?" Emily realized the question was blunt, but better to get the hard stuff out early. Maggie sighed. She had been anticipating this question, she had in fact asked the very same of her own mother, just the day before. It was a natural question to ask, and she knew the answer would be unsatisfying to the intense young woman standing next to her.

"Just some guy I met on a trip to Europe after college. He was French, and I loved how he said my name, with his accent, pronouncing every syllable and rolling the r's." She paused and pronounced her name as he had...her eyes closed as if he were standing right in front of her.

"Magarrrriiittt."

"We stayed together for three months. When I had to return to the states, that was it. I came back with a souvenir though," she paused and looked at Emily, "...you."

"And no," she rushed to continue, "we are not in touch. Wouldn't know how to reach him, as I never really had a last name that I trusted. I guess the Teach women always have been inclined towards rogues."

"Did you love him?" Emily asked.

"Well...yes and no. I loved the idea of him, the adventure, the danger, the exotic flavor of it. But in the end did I love him? No. He was selfish and narcissistic and had no interest in a future with me, with us." She smiled at her daughter.

"So, tell me about your young man. How did you meet? Are you dating or?" she left off the rest.

Emily didn't know how to respond. Hearing Mark described as her young man was odd. She didn't think of them as a couple, after their one night together they hadn't seen each other until Emily showed up at the funeral home to tell him he had fathered a child. Could they be a couple? Emily was afraid to answer that question for herself.

Mark was good looking, confident, popular. Everything Emily felt she wasn't. Even if she were interested in something more, she couldn't imagine he would give her a second look. She was invisible. She dressed to blend in, to be one of the guys at work. While she rationalized that it was to aid her career prospects, she suspected that she'd try to blend in, chameleon-like, in any situation.

"At a bar…he's a musician; I saw him playing and waited until the band was done. His name is Mark."

Tears erupted. Stung her eyes then slid in hot streaks down her cheeks. It was a cry she had held off until this moment. Hot tears held the shame and embarrassment of her predicament in a life that had been otherwise predictable, responsible. They were alone on the ship now and Emily turned to face her mother. Maggie put her arm around her daughter's shoulder and Emily heaved great sobs. She cried until there were no more tears; until the shame had washed out.

"I can't believe it happened, it's so unlike me."

"Is it really? You've just met thirteen generations of women from the same family, and all have the same story. I think it might be entirely like you."

Emily thought about that and felt the tension leave her shoulders.

"Maggie, have you ever been in love, really in love?"

132

"Yes, at least I think so."

"How did you know?"

"Nothing else seemed to matter but him and us," her mother replied, "Emily dear, are you in love?"

"I really don't know."

"Does the father know about the baby?"

"I had just told him before going to the tea shop. He didn't freak out, so that's good. Please don't say anything to anyone else. I don't want anyone to know."

"If you wish," Maggie smiled. "We'd best go to shore. We can continue talking later." Emily nodded and turned to climb over the railing. She stopped and looked at her biological mother, whose auburn hair matched Emily's perfectly.

"One more question," Emily wasn't really sure she wanted the answer, "are you still alive?" Maggie pondered the question and answered the only way she could.

"I don't know. I suppose it depends on when you are talking about."

"In my time."

"Yes, assuming we all survive this."

CHAPTER EIGHTEEN

EMILY

Emily awoke to a star-filled sky, arched over the beach like the ceiling of a cathedral. After talking well into the night, the women finally fell asleep on the sand, grouped around campfires.

Every available spec of the black sky was full of stars and even so, there was more black sky. Slowly she lifted her head and looked around. She was the only one awake and she took the sound of soft snoring from among the prone bodies as proof. Bedalia was gone. Moving carefully so as not to wake anyone, she stood and picked her way around arms and legs to reach open sand.

The stars reflected on the gentle waves, making the water sparkle as it rippled against the sand. The darkness along the horizon was startlingly black, no cities in the distance casting light into the sky. Emily dipped her foot into the water and felt its warmth. Nothing like the Atlantic she was familiar with, which held onto the cold of winter far too long. Relishing her private time in this magical never-land she swung her arms out and twirled in place, stopping when her arms encircled her own shoulders in a hug, her eyes closed. This world of oceans and women was wonderful, and she was beginning to wish she didn't have to return to her own rushed existence. She could stay here forever, suspended in time, and never have to face the decision of what to do with the baby.

The baby, she repeated in her mind, my baby. What am I going to do with a baby? Will I be able to work, will my adopted Mom help, or will she disown me? Will my baby have a father? Without agonizing over it her thoughts were not on whether to keep the baby but on how to care for it. Who would be in its life? And then there was the biggest wild card, Mark, with his penetrating blue eyes, wispy blond hair, and athletic build. Her heart felt tight when she thought of him, was that love? Is a lifetime decision made on a physical feeling of tightness in the chest? To Emily's rational mind that didn't make sense. Yet there was no denying the fact that the more she thought of him, his caring concern when she told him she was pregnant, his offer to support her however she chose to proceed, all made her want to be with him more. To talk and plan. Is that love?

"It is pretty, no?" came the soft mocha voice. Emily opened her eyes, knowing who she would see and annoyed at having her private moment interrupted.

"Yes, it is," she replied guardedly.

"In your time this is a secluded beach for a hotel, a small but charming hotel."

"That's sad. This beach should remain unspoiled." She tried to imagine someone cutting the trees towering at the edge of the jungle ninety feet away to make a hotel. It made her wince.

"You are sensitive to the thought," Bedalia observed, "I sensed you were in tune."

"In tune? In tune with what?" Part of her knew the answer.

She remembered the night on the ship when she had seen into Bedalia's thoughts. Emily had sensed anger and jealousy through the brilliant rush of colors. Tonight though, she felt a calmness come from Bedalia.

"In tune with the energies of the planet, of the universe." Bedalia swept her hand to point to the earth, sky, trees, and water.

Emily looked at the woman, noting that her eyes were shining brightly, more brightly than the moonlight should have allowed. For the first time, she noticed how tall Bedalia was, the darkness masking the bright clothing she wore.

"Who are you?" Emily asked. It was a question that had been on her mind since she left the tea shop.

"I am a traveler, just like you."

Emily looked at the mysterious woman. That answer didn't help her, yet asking again didn't seem like the right approach, so she chose silence as a strategy.

"Mary and you are the most in-tune of the group. It is because you and Mary are bookends of energy that I was able to find you all, spread out over time like you were." Bedalia turned and stared out at the water, Emily followed her lead and the two watched the water flow in and out.

"Where are you traveling from or to?" Emily finally asked.

"From here to there, from in to out. Same as you do in your dreams, I'm just more," she paused, looking for the right word, "purposeful in my travels,"

"I don't understand."

"Love."

"Love? What is that really?" Emily asked.

Bedalia smiled a glowing, white-toothed smile.

"Love is all there is really. It comes in many shades, hues, and intensities. It is the strongest substance in the universe. It binds thoughts together into worlds and creates everything you know. When that energy is channeled toward one person it draws us to them, allows us to see their good beyond their faults, makes us feel stronger when we are with them."

"Love is the strongest energy there is. I love Ed and want him with me. I'm directing that love energy to help you so you can help him. It is simple, really."

"So that's how this is all possible? All of us here?"

"Aye, it is. Mary is fearful that anything will undo the spell. She doesn't understand it isn't a spell; all your lives exist now and, in the past, and future. The ship merely exists in all. It sounds simple, but it does take some doing. There is much your scientists don't understand yet."

"Is that how we survived the maelstrom?"

"Yes, that too."

Emily turned to look at the dark horizon and shimmering water.

"What about Mary? Couldn't your love energy protect her? What will happen to her?"

"Mary will be fine," Bedalia said, just as if she had said the weather tomorrow will be fine. Emily wasn't sure what to say. She wanted to yell at the woman, shake her for getting her family involved, and putting Mary in jeopardy. Yet it was because of this woman that she had met her mother, grandmother, and great-grandmother. If this was all a dream, she didn't want to wake up until she got to the end of the story.

"Why are you doing it?"

"I've told you already. Because I fell in love. Nothing more. Is it so hard to believe that someone could love Ed Teach?" A brief wind blew Emily's hair.

"No, I guess not," Emily turned to look at Bedalia, but she was gone, vanished as if she had never been there.

CHAPTER NINETEEN

MARY

Mary awoke alone. Mist dripping from the leaves of her hiding spot. Gently pulling a leaf to the side she saw a sight that made her heart skip. The cove was empty. True to his word, Hornigold had abandoned her on an island. He expected her to die here, something she had no intention of doing. But would intention serve her well enough to survive?

She had never had to forage for her own food or build her own shelter. She took the large leaf that was dripping and fashioned a funnel and drank some of the condensed water. Her stomach growled.

Her shelter for the night had been just feet from the sand. In the dark, it had felt much further like she had pushed far more leaves away than she did. The excitement of the storm and her capture had exhausted her, and despite being wet from her swim she had fallen right to sleep. Sleeping in a curled-up ball left her stiff and sore.

Mary fingered the key she had taken to wearing on a leather cord around her neck. Despite the closeness to her skin, the metal felt cool. This key has brought me here, she thought, introduced me to my daughter, and caused Hornigold to hunt me. Why didn't he kill me? Probably power and fear, the two primary motivators of men. I'm sure he believes himself to have such a great power over me that I couldn't help but tell him the truth. But really, he should be afraid; *The Maryann* grows stronger each day.

Since opening the lock to the tower door on St. Thomas, Mary had kept the key on her, magnetically attracted to its heft and strength. She tucked it back beneath her tunic and stood, stretching her arms over her head as if to defy Hornigold, who was long gone. The jungle was alive with the sounds of birds. A gentle breeze blew plant fronds from side to side. They made scratching sounds that sounded like animals crawling through the dense undergrowth.

Her clothes were still damp, but the air was muggy and warm and the fact that she was wet seemed to help her stay cooler. The sun was just starting to rise, and Mary knew that it would be hot shortly, and she needed to find something to eat before she sought shelter somewhere cooler. A higher elevation would help.

The humidity slowed her down. The air felt heavy on her skin, as if it had as much substance as the plants she pushed her way through. The vegetation was so thick, towering over Mary's head that she had no clear sense of direction and therefore was surprised and dismayed when she found herself back where she had started. What seemed like hours had been spent going in one large circle. Mary sat on the ground, sweat pouring down her face. It was only dawn and already too hot. She needed to get down to the water, where the going would be easier, and a way to higher elevation would hopefully be easier to find. She angled down toward the water.

As she walked, she made as much noise as possible, and birdsong stopped as she approached. After an hour of thrashing through the plants, some as tall as she was, she found a plant that bore a pendulous fruit that smelled heavenly. She poked her fingernail through the surface and sticky juice flowed out.

This couldn't be poisonous she thought, berries or leaves are poisonous but not sweet fruit. The sweetness draws animals to eat it and carry its seeds to other places. Poison would be counterproductive, so she bit it. Juice ran down her face and the flavor exploded with sweetness in her mouth. She didn't know how long it would take for any poison to take effect so after finishing the fruit she sat down to wait. After a wait of what seemed like an hour with no effects she stood and picked a few more fruits to fill her stomach.

This won't be so hard she thought, I can get water from the leaves and fruit from the tree.

Mary could swear she smelled coffee as she finished the last of the fruits she had picked. Was she hallucinating from the fruit? No, that was coffee she smelled. Coffee meant civilization.

Headhunters and island dwellers didn't drink coffee, Mary was sure of it.

She thrashed through the brush noisily to scare away any predators or slimy things hidden among the large leaves. The air was heavy and hot as she pushed her way through the brush, following a line about one hundred feet from the shore.

The path eventually took her to the next cove over. When she tumbled out from the brush onto the sandy beach, she couldn't believe her eyes. There anchored safely in the cove was *The Maryann* and strewn about the beach, mostly asleep, were her family. They had somehow survived the same storm, and her ruse with Hornigold had worked. It had worked so well in fact; he had abandoned her on the very same island *The Maryann* sought.

"Hello!" she called out. "You can't imagine how happy I am to see you."

CHAPTER TWENTY

EMILY

Emily slept fitfully after her talk with Bedalia. She woke early when the smell of coffee reached her and penetrated the fog in her head. Henry was moving quietly around a fire built in a wood stove in the kitchen. He held out a cup of the steaming black liquid as she approached.

"Thanks," she held the mug in both hands, breathing in its pungent aroma. The steam itself was a good stimulant.

"Henry, I didn't see you asleep on the beach last night."

"Aye, I went back to the ship. Someone needs to be aboard in case she slipped her mooring."

"Oh. Thanks. I guess we didn't think of that."

"Well, you're not exactly skilled sailors." Emily looked at him and couldn't tell whether he was trying to insult or just stating a fact.

"Yes, you're right."

"Henry, why are you here? You're the only man in a crew of women. We're all related by blood, or I guess in Bedalia's case, by love, to Blackbeard. How do you fit in?"

Henry picked up a long stick and poked at the embers, stirring them into a small flame.

"Eddy was my brother. I came from England to bring him home, away from the person he was becoming. Only I was too late. Maynard killed him before I arrived. He was my baby brother."

Emily opened her mouth to speak but nothing came out. The idea of a family in England worrying about the deeds of Blackbeard had never occurred to her. The idea of a monster like Blackbeard being someone's little brother, or son, turned everything upside down.

"Bedalia asked for my help. It seemed the right thing to do."

"So, you're my great uncle?"

"Keep that to yourself, will you, I haven't told Mary yet."

"Why not?"

He scratched his chin. "My brother could be a bit rough. I suspect she doesn't pine for him."

That was an understatement. Emily nodded in agreement. This new piece of information gave her something to think about. She wandered away from the fire with her cup of coffee, and so was the first to hear a large animal thrashing in the jungle and coming toward them. Foolishly, she now thought, they had left the swords on the deck of the ship and looking around the only weapon they had was the cup of steaming hot coffee. Emily held out the make-shift weapon, ready to throw its contents on whatever came out of the jungle. The sounds increased until at last a figure emerged. Emily almost dropped the cup; she was so surprised.

"Mary! You're alive!" Her scream woke the others. When they saw Mary, they too began to scream and run toward her. Mary took a few steps forward in the sand and collapsed. Her granddaughters lifted her and carried her to the nearest fire and set her down on a blanket. After loading a plate high with food and getting her a nice hot cup of coffee they sat around her to hear what happened.

"We thought we'd lost you. Where were you?"

Mary swallowed a bit of food and smiled.

"I could say the same thing of you. After the storm, *The Maryann* and the other four boats were gone. I didn't know what to think. Hornigold kidnapped me to get the map. Fortunately, I didn't have it with me. He made me point to the island on the map, but I pointed to one far from here. Hopefully, he's well on his way to Jamaica and has yet to realize what a fool he was. It is too bad I didn't have my handbag with me, I could have put that pistol to effective use."

"How did you get to this island?" Emily asked.

"Hornigold left me here, hoping I will die. They all got very drunk, and I escaped. I've never been fond of drink, but as I sit here, I'm grateful they had lots on board and tried to drink it all. He didn't realize he'd dropped anchor off the very island he sought."

"I guess Bedalia's magic doesn't extend to protecting us aboard the ship. This journey is more dangerous than I thought it would be." Mary chuckled. "I did surprise myself at how easily I deceived the captain into thinking that the treasure island was far away. Now that we are here, let's all eat and then find this treasure."

Emily thought back to her conversation last night with Bedalia. She wasn't so sure that Bedalia's magic had limitations. This seemed proof that her magic was indeed strong.

They all agreed to tackle finding the treasure after a hearty breakfast of eggs. The chickens, who were grateful for having survived the storm, had laid a generous quantity of brown, speckled eggs.

Emily drifted away from the group, walking down to put her toes in the water. The waves washed up gently against the shore, the sand sugar white and soft. Emily stood quietly, taking in the morning. Did last night happen? Had she spoken with Bedalia or was that just a vivid dream? She scrunched her toes in the sand and felt the coolness of the damper sand deeper down.

Yes, there she saw it, a footprint. She quickly stepped to the small print and compared the arch and width. It was hers all right, but was it from last night, or had she left it there when they landed? She scanned the horizon for signs of another ship. She wasn't as convinced as Mary that Hornigold had been fooled into thinking the island he sought was far in another direction. Did he know Bedalia was helping them? Emily thought about Bedalia's death on this island. That was why Bedalia had been more like a spirit last night, this is her return to the scene of the crime. Her spirit was strongest here.

In the morning light, they could see the white sand beach extend for about a mile, ending at the edge of a thick jungle of trees, tall palms, and bushy ferns. Trekking through the dense vegetation would be difficult and not one she thought they were prepared for. All the women were finishing their breakfast as she returned to the group.

"Bedalia, how do we cut through the dense brush? Is there a trail to follow or do we have to make our own?" Emily asked.

"None exists; you will need to cut your trail." Her eyes were shining brightly, but not with the same glowing as last night. It must have been the moon or something Emily thought. Henry began rummaging around in the pile of kitchen utensils they had lugged from the ship and pulled out a machete, a long, thickly curved, and menacing-looking blade.

"I can't help you find the treasure, although I do know where it is. See if you can find a starting point in the brush. You will need to head up the mountain," Bedalia was pointing to the volcanic-looking peak in the middle of the largest segment of the island, "don't go too fast though, and stick together."

Emily nodded. There was no telling who or what else could be on this island besides them. Her imagination could envision cannibals, bushmen, huge gorillas, and throwback reptiles that no one has ever seen. A gun would be more protection than the old machete Henry had just given her.

"Should we go back to the ship and get more swords or Mary's pistol?"

"You will be fine with the machete," Bedalia assured them.

"Henry, are you coming with us?" Emily asked. He had asked her to keep his identity quiet for now.

"No. I'll stay with the ship." Emily nodded. She wasn't sure why he wasn't eager to hunt for treasure, although his bad leg would slow them down, and she liked the idea of having someone watch the ship. Without *The Maryann,* there didn't seem any way to return to her real life, a life that was so far away as a dream.

"Mary," Emily called out, "are you ready to start?" Mary nodded slowly.

"Yes, I'm ready. We are getting closer; I can feel it in my bones." She stood and pulled down on her tunic. Emily noticed a degree of confidence in Mary that had not been there before.

"Leave the cups," Bedalia said, "I won't be going with you. I'll clean them and Henry and I will pack things up."

"Why won't you come with us?"

"Remember, this is your treasure Mary, yours to find and yours to take. You need to rely on family ties to accomplish this, family ties."

Emily walked over to Mary and handed her the machete. Mary took the heavy blade, and stepping back from the group, swung it a few times. Emily wondered if Mary suspected that Henry was family, her brother-in-law.

"I suppose anywhere is as good a place to start," Mary walked up to a leafy spot between two trees and started swinging the machete. Ann followed her closely behind, and without planning, the rest of the women fell behind her in chronological order.

The trail wasn't very wide, and the plants seemed to close in around Emily as she moved forward. The path disappeared behind her; the warmth of the sun gave way to the cooler air of the jungle as they went deeper into the shade. What else was in this jungle with them, she wondered. How much danger were they in from wild beasts and wild men?

CHAPTER TWENTY-ONE

EMILY

The path angled uphill from the moment they entered the jungle brush. Despite the initial coolness of the shade, the humidity and heat increased with each step up the mountain. As the morning wore on Emily could feel her pulse throb in the blood that rushed through her face.

Their progress was halting, Mary would stop and start whacking at the large leaves and stems that blocked the path and when a large enough passageway formed the women would follow her quietly until she stopped and started hacking again. Emily lost count of how many times the process had repeated, starting to think of ways to make the chopping more efficient through time and motion studies. The procession finally stopped in front of a cave opening wide enough for them to slip through.

The cave looked exactly like Emily had dreamed it would be. This fact was disquieting to her. Maggie leaned back and spoke over her shoulder.

"Didn't you dream about a cave?" Emily nodded.

"What other dreams did you have?" she whispered as they stared at the cave.

Large fan-shaped palm leaves guarded the entrance. Mary used the machete to hack back the branches and give them access. Now that they could see the cave's arched, stony, opening they could also see a shrunken head swinging by its hair from the top of the arch, just like in her dream. The head looked hauntingly familiar, but Emily couldn't place it.

If it matched her dream, a glass door or force field blocked the opening.

Ann stepped forward. "Blackbeard was my father, I'll go first."

As Ann moved to enter the cave, Mary called out to her, "Wait, I'll go with you. It's because of me we are all here, isn't it?"

It was she who had suffered the abuse of Blackbeard. It was she who had the key, sat in the tower, and solved the riddle. The two women held hands and proceeded to walk forward. They didn't go far before they bounced back from an invisible shield. The wind blew through the space as if nothing were there, yet when Ann put her hand up to push through whatever had stopped them, she met a resistance that held her hand in place.

"What sort of magic is this?" Mary asked the group. It was the opening Emily had been looking for. She had inexplicitly known since setting foot on the island that there would be an obstacle and a password needed to enter the cave, and she had known what the password must be. She moved up to the front of the line from her place two from the rear. When she got to the front, she examined the opening.

"Good question. In the movies," she held up her hand to pre-1900s women, "I'll explain that later, but in the movies when there was a magic door there was a password, something like 'abracadabra'. Can anyone think of a password that Blackbeard might have used to block the entrance to this cave?" she paused for dramatic effect; because she was sure she knew.

Winnie was the first to speak. "I thought Bedalia said they never found the treasure. If that is true, why would he put a curse and password on the cave?" The general murmuring of 'good point,' and 'yes, I heard that too,' followed her question. The dream was coming back to Emily now. She was sure that Blackbeard had found the cave but hadn't shared that news with Hornigold or even Bedalia that fateful night on the beach when they fought and Bedalia had died.

She turned to face the dangling, shrunken head. Could that have been a human? Taking a deep breath, she spoke to the head.

"Bedalia!"

It began swinging wildly as if a strong breeze off the ocean was now hitting it directly. Emily would swear for years after that the shrunken head's eyes winked at her. Emily took this as a sign that the invisible blockade was now gone, and she confidently moved towards the entrance. There was a gasp as she passed through.

"I had a dream about a cave and a head. Bedalia was the password in my dream, it was worth a try," she explained.

"There is one possible theory," Maggie spoke loudly, staring at the shrunken head. The women turned to look at her.

"And what is that?" Mary asked.

Maggie pointed to the shriveled head, still swaying from its leather cord. "That could be Bedalia." Heads snapped around to look at the head, Mary nodded in agreement.

"I could see that, she's the guardian of the cave and by extension the treasure. To release her and him, the treasure needs to pass on. She said she can't help us, though she's helped us all get here, we survived the storm and my kidnapping. Her magic is strong."

Emily turned and placed her hands on the stone arch, feeling the cool dampness and soft fuzziness of the dark lichens and mold growing on the surface. Her heartbeat quickly in her chest, nervous about the discovery and apprehensive at what they might find. Not that most pirate movies she'd ever seen were realistic, however, they had planted notions about what to expect, and none of them were good. They were going to go into this cave in search of treasure. At what risk was she placing her baby? Although she hadn't decided to keep it, increasingly it felt real.

"All it needs is the ABANDON ALL HOPE YE WHO ENTER HERE sign," Maggie said as she came up behind Emily. Her joking words brought Emily back to the present. The baby decision would have to wait for some quiet time.

"Are we all ready?" Mary called out.

"Yes!" everyone answered, and she turned and walked slowly into the mouth of the cave, the shrunken head still swinging madly.

It was cool and dark inside, the walls damp from the trapped humidity and a trickle of water here and there seeping through the rocks above. The dank air smelled of minerals and darkness.

Mary reached the first turn in the tunnel using the light from the cave's entrance and as total darkness swallowed her, Emily, at the end of the line, entered the mouth of the cave. Suddenly a flash of yellow light filled the cave and in the light of the flame, Emily saw Mary triumphantly holding a torch held high in her hand.

"I figured every self-respecting pirate would leave something to light the way to their treasure," she explained, smiling, "so I used my flint again, a very handy thing to have around."

Looks like Hollywood got that one right, Emily thought, and if they got that right, what else did they get right?

The sound of all the women's footsteps and her own breath was all that Emily could hear. She strained to hear warning sounds of danger, although she wasn't sure what they would be. Bats, or signs that this old volcanic peak was coming to life. To a woman, the unknowingness of the darkness instilled fear, and none spoke.

157

The procession slowly made its way into the rocky cave for what seemed like hours, before Mary stopped and let the stragglers catch up. Emily, who was last in line behind Maggie, saw that they had entered a dome roofed grotto with a small circular window at the top of the cave, a glimmer of sunlight working its way through brush growing around the sphincter at the opening at the top of the dome.

Clear, fresh water was trickling through the hole into a pool at the bottom of the cavern. The water was dark, foreboding, and blocked their progress to the tunnel which Emily could barely see on the other side. A rocky ledge gave some tentative footing partway around the lake, but not far enough to reach the other side.

To cross it they would have to use a boat, swim, or even swing over it. In the dim light, Emily could see that there was no boat, and nothing to use as a swing over the water. Reaching down she put her hand in the water, cool and fresh.

"We swam to the island from the ship, no reason we can't swim across this pool," Ann offered. "might make our clothes feel better. Mine are caked with salt."

The air in the grotto was warm. Staring at the lake, Mary periodically took the torch and held it out as far as she could reach, peering down into the water. Ripples from the drips falling into the grotto spread out, crossing over one another creating a variable cross-hatched pattern on the surface of the dark water. It looked safe enough Emily thought.

Isabel stepped forward, "I want to go first. I love to swim, and this is just like a lake at the rock quarry near where I grew up. I'm not afraid."

Everyone but Mary stepped back to let Isabel lead the way. Mary was still staring at the water, her left arm holding aloft the torch, her right arm stretched out to block anyone from entering the water. Undeterred, Isabel she sat on the edge of the rocky pool and slid herself in. "It is lovely!" she called out and began to use the breaststroke to cross the pool. Ripples from her arms spread and mingled with the circles from the dripping water creating new patterns of water and light.

It happened so quickly that no one saw what it was. Isabel was there one minute and gone the next, pulled under the water's surface by something large and snakelike which slapped a tail and disappeared.

Thirteen women screamed in unison, the sound reverberating around the stone cavern.

Without a moment's hesitation or rational thought, Emily pushed her way to the edge and jumped into the water, swimming to the spot where Isabel had disappeared. Years of lifeguard training kicked in and her eyes never left the spot where Isabel had gone down.

She reached down and began waving her arm under the water's surface searching for Isabel's hand. When that didn't work Emily dove, returning to the surface seconds later pulling Isabel's arm. She gasped for air as soon as her head shot above water.

Everyone called for them to get out of the water quickly and Emily did strong kicks which got them to the edge and out in time to see the immense, snake-like thing slide past, disappointed to have lost its prey.

Isabel was thanking Emily profusely, apologizing for all the bother. Emily just nodded and labored to catch her breath. Her fear of the cave was growing. First the password, then the torch, and now a sea monster, what was next - booby traps and poison-tipped darts?

"What happened Isabel, did it let you go?" Mary asked as she helped to stabilize the woman.

Isabel nodded her head. "It just grabbed my legs and pulled me under, I was so frightened I fainted, so maybe it thought I was dead and didn't want me anymore. Just as Emily reached me, it let go."

Mary looked at Emily gratefully, "Thank you, Emily, I believe you saved Isabel's life."

"It was nothing," Emily was sure she had nothing to do with it. Bedalia's magic had saved them again.

"Oh yes it was!" came a chorus of voices.

"Well, we certainly can't swim across. Is there any way across which we can float?" Mary asked.

Emily shook her head. She had been thoroughly scanning the lake and the tunnel.

"The tunnel isn't wide enough to bring a boat through, and the driftwood on the island isn't strong enough to support a person without dragging bits of themselves in the water. I supposed we could go and scrounge up all the driftwood we can find or scavenge some of the wood from the ship and make a raft, we can ferry the group across with. Other than that, the only way I see across is through the lake."

"I read a story once," Isadora said loudly, "that had a water monster like ours." "They used music to soothe the beast and get past it."

Mary snorted. "Music? On that thing?" She pointed to the water.

"It nearly killed Isabel!"

"We don't have musical instruments," said Caroline. She seemed unperturbed by the monster.

"Sure, we do," said Elizabeth, "we have our voices."

Heads nodded in concurrence and they began a heated discussion on what song they would sing. Given the large generational differences between them all, the only song that was universally known was Rock a Bye Baby.

Caroline gave a starting note and they all hummed it to themselves. The humming sound grew in the grotto as one by one they all found the note and joined in. The solid rock walls once again echoed with sound and the grotto vibrated with the energy of the one note. As the sound energy penetrated her chest a feeling of connectedness filled Emily. The sound united her with the women around her, her family, something she thought she'd never experience, and people she never expected to know, and her baby.

161

Her quest for her birth mother had yielded a bounty of mothers, grandmothers, and great grandmothers. She put her arm around the nearest woman, Elizabeth, and the two women leaned their heads together, which made the effect even greater. Elizabeth in turn put her arm around Madeline and within minutes all fourteen women were in a circle with their arms around each other, a circle of family with no beginning and no end, the humming sound traveling around and around the grotto, building on itself until it sounded like a huge choir.

Emily looked up from the tight circle of women with their heads together and saw the immense water-snake rise to the surface listening to the music. Its slippery skin shone in the light of the flame and the tiny bit of sun that dropped through the opening at the top. Yellow eyes with ink-black slits sought the source of the soothing sound as the snake swam the perimeter of the pool looking unsuccessfully for the point of origin, the humming sound feeding upon itself and filling every crevice with the one note, now a chord as it shifted tone in its endless trips within the dome.

Unable to find whatever was making the sound, the sea monster drifted to one side of the lake and laid its head on the rocky shore, closing its huge eyes and listening. Emily gently laid her hand on Mary's shoulder and drew her attention to the beast, now still, its eyes closed as if in sleep. She motioned with her arms to Mary and the rest to keep humming and she felt around with her foot until she found a small stone, which she tossed into the pool as close to the snake as she dared. The splash was barely

162

audible over the humming and the snake did not stir. Emily turned back to Mary and using hand signals tried to indicate they should keep humming and at the same time, quietly swim across the pool on the side opposite the snake. The circle of women mimicked back to her the swimming motion she used with her hands to indicate their comprehension, and with Mary in the lead, they slowly lowered themselves into the water along the side furthest from the snake, still resting, entranced by the sound.

Mary swam holding the torch high, afraid that if it got wet it wouldn't start again. Emily could swear she saw a smile on the snake's scaly face and marveled again at what the circle of women could do. It took fifteen long minutes to get them across, Emily coming across last and almost disturbing the beast as she struggled to get out of the pond. Once clear of the water and further into the tunnel the humming slowly died out.

"That worked!" Mary said.

They were wet from their swim, but the tunnel floor was wetter, a trickle of water was following them from the lake. As they moved further, water seeping down the walls joined the trickle and it grew in depth and width.

"The lake is draining through this tunnel stream," Emily observed, "maybe there's another way out and we won't have to deal with the snake."

"I hope you're right." The tunnel was dark the women linked hands to stay together. Emily again brought up the rear. The water at their feet trickled along with them, gradually building as the slope of the tunnel dipped down, the force and volume of water making it harder to stand. It wasn't long before the water was up to their knees.

CHAPTER TWENTY-TWO

MARY

Sarah shouted from the back of the line.

"Where is all this water coming from?"

"Seeping through the rocks or other grottos like the one we just came from," came another voice from further back in the line, although Mary couldn't identify its owner. Wet rocky walls and the soft shushing sound coming from further down the tunnel distorted sound.

Her ears were barely detecting the muffled sound, but she noticed that it was getting louder as they progressed along the tunnel. The light from the torch grew brighter as the column of marchers entered another grotto.

A dry ledge diverted to the left, and the trickle of water that had grown into a small river ran down the right side of the grotto. The ledge widened as they walked along. Torchlight shone brightly off a long narrow boat which lay careened on its side beside the underground river as if it were waiting for them.

"Will that boat fit through the tunnel back into the lake?" Mary asked, thinking they may not have to swim through the snake lake after all.

"I don't think so," Emily replied, "Although maybe we can take it apart and rebuild it there."

"This water is going somewhere," Maggie observed, peering down to where the river re-entered a tunnel. "My guess is there is another way out."

Mary's eyes strained in the darkness to see an alternate path across the river, the peril she was putting this group through was all her doing, and she was keenly aware that if anything happened, it would be her fault. Her fault for following the lure of the key, her fault for allowing Bedalia to magic them all here, and her fault for asking them to find the treasure for her.

She had not spent much time thinking about it, yet now it hit her with full force, what would happen to the women and the treasure? Her visions didn't include any of them going back to their own times with treasure.

The treasure was hers, bought with suffering at the hands of a brutal and devious husband. The idea that she would share was foreign, she had never had to share anything with anyone in her life. She was an only child and therefore had no hand-me-downs to contend with and no little sister or brother to split time with her father. No, the treasure was hers.

166

Ann squeezed past her mother to get closer to the boat to help push. Mary stood still, feeling the sensation of pressure on her skin where her daughter had brushed past. How does one grasp the information that you have a daughter when you've completely dismissed the idea out of hand? Do you open your heart and let her in, no questions asked, or keep her at a safe distance, questioning the truth of the situation? Mary had not resolved that in the days on the ship. She watched Ann climb the ropes without a mother's concern for her child's safety. She watched Ann sit and talk with the woman who was her child without a grandmother's curiosity.

The group of women had moved around the small boat and Mary realized she was about to be left behind in her haze of thought.

With everyone helping, the boat moved to the river, and with its flat bottom, it bobbed neatly in the shallow waters. One by one they crawled in and sat down. Miraculously it held them all.

"I don't see oars or a rudder. How do we steer?" Emily asked. Mary used the torch to survey the flat landing where the boat had lain but found no oars or other boating accessories.

"I guess we let the current take us, and the channel is too narrow to worry about steering."

"Ah," said Isadora, "so this is like the boat in the Tunnel of Love at Coney Island."

Maggie winked at Emily and Caroline as the boat began moving on the current, entering another tunnel. The little ship picked up speed, and Mary could tell they were going slightly downhill. The entrance to the cave had been a hefty hike up the mountainous island, so going downhill didn't alarm her. The wind began to rush past her ears as the steepness of the decline accelerated and the boat picked up speed.

Short shrieks and nervous laughter came from behind her, but nothing escaped her lips. As they continued to pick up speed, the wind blew out Mary's torch.

Women screamed, and raw fear now gripped Mary's chest as her heart leaped wildly, as if to escape the out-of-control boat. She held on to the sides of the boat tightly and her voice joined the screams of the rest when suddenly the bottom of the boat seemed to drop out from under them and they plunged into the darkness. Someone behind her moaned in pain and she yelled back over her shoulder to hold on, regardless of how much it hurt.

With a jolt the ship leaned to the right as the tunnel turned, splashing cool water into the boat. The side of the boat dipped hard and Mary's fingers felt the water as she held on to the sides with every ounce of energy she had.

Her inner ear told her they were going in circles as the boat continued to turn, and turn and turn, further plunging into the mountain. Nausea built in her stomach and above the fear of falling through a dark mountain passage to who knows what, the cold chill of seasickness and the vile taste of vomit rose in her throat. Now is not the time, she told herself repeatedly as the boat

168

barreled ahead. With a whoosh of chilly air, the boat spit out of the tunnel and reached deeper water.

CHAPTER TWENTY-THREE

EMILY

The boat slowed quickly when it hit the deeper water. They must be in another cavern, Emily thought, though in this one the darkness was complete. There were no cracks in the ceiling for sunlight to sneak through and light their way. She could hear Mary unsuccessfully trying to light the torch again with a wet piece of flint.

"Where are we?" Ann asked with a strained voice, and Emily guessed that it was her that had been moaning.

"Everyone all right?" she asked cheerfully. Then with a whoosh, the torch roared into flame again and cheers erupted. They were in another cavern with another lake. This lake had a shore big enough to get out onto, and on the shore, gleaming in the light of the flame, was a vast pile of gold objects, Blackbeard's treasure.

Using their hands, carefully, for they remembered the great snake in the first lake, they paddled over to the shore and climbed out, one at a time, then pulled the boat out of the water to prevent it from floating away.

The pile of treasure was as tall as the tallest of them, and twenty yards wide, a mountainous pile of gold and jewels.

"Where did he get all this?" Caroline asked.

"Remember Bedalia told us this is the lost treasure of Captain Henry Morgan after a raid on Panama," Mary walked around looking at the variety of objects that made up the pile. Her pile. They had found the treasure and it was as magnificent as she had hoped.

"How long ago was that?" Caroline asked, "Shouldn't we give it back?"

"Give it back?" Mary's voice screeched. "Give it back to the Spanish? No, the King of Spain doesn't deserve it, he raped the countryside to get it, and they killed our sailors and soldiers. This is spoils of war, forgotten to time, and we have now found it, it is ours." She held back from saying "It is mine." Without them, she would never have found this. Reluctantly she realized she would have to share it.

"We can't carry this all back at one time," Elizabeth said, "it's too much."

Emily walked over to pick up a chalice, made of pure gold. It was cool and soft to the touch and very heavy. The golden cup glowed in the torchlight.

"She's right, too much of this, and the boat will sink," she observed, carefully setting the cup back on the pile. "And unless there is another exit, we still haven't figured out how to get out of the mountain, and that snake will eventually grow resistant to the sound of our humming, so we probably have one go at it to get out whatever we want." The group reluctantly realized the logic and began to circle the pile of jewels and gold to decide what they wanted to take back. It was like a great sale at the shopping mall, with women grabbing at jeweled necklaces, looping them around their necks, and holding as many objects in their arms as possible.

At last, silence settled on the group. The women were clutching their treasure, looking guilty for what they had taken and regretful that they couldn't carry more. Mary held the most as if determined to leave as little as possible behind.

"All right, now we have a decision to make," Emily said, stepping forward. "Do we try to go back the way we came, or...," she pointed at an opening in the cave wall just visible beyond the torchlight, "...or do we keep going in the direction of the river?"

As one they answered, "Keep going," Emily shook her head and laughed. She came from an adventurous stock.

"Keep going it is - All aboard!"

When they had what they could safely carry and themselves loaded into the boat, the pile of jewels and chains of gold looked barely touched. Emily figured that each of them was thinking what she was thinking. She'd come back here in her own time and recover what was left. That snake couldn't live forever. The boat began moving slowly in the current, weighted down with the heavy treasure. When they again began to slope down, gravity pulled harder and harder on the gold as if to reclaim it. The boat began to pick up speed and Emily could hear golden objects drop to the floor of the boat as the women freed their hands to hold on for dear life once again. They turned a sharp right corner, nearly swamping the boat and Emily noticed the smell of the air change; salty and fresh.

Up ahead at the front of the boat she heard Mary cry out and the boat plunged into darkness. A few seconds later Emily understood why, as she passed under a waterfall dropping more fresh water into the river. With the added liquid, the gold, jewels, and fourteen people the boat was now riding so low that the water line was mere inches from the edge.

One more waterfall and we'll sink, thought Emily.

Despite the low drafting and the cargo of people, treasure, and water the boat continued to pick up speed and was traveling quite fast when a burst of light hit them.

The boat shot out of the tunnel into mid-air and plummeted to the sea below. The fall felt slow motion compared to the speed they had been traveling inside the tunnel, and the rush of fresh, warm air was momentarily exhilarating and then quickly horrifying. Boat and women separated, gold and jewels spread out as the total assemblage fell thirty yards to the surging water below.

They crashed into the sea and bounced off the jagged volcanic rocks at its base. Emily hit the water hard, tumbling as she sank, losing her orientation and feeling the rise of panic as she realized she couldn't tell up from down.

Her lungs were burning as she looked around, finally seeing the bottom of the boat against the brightness of the sky and swam frantically back to the surface. The water was warmer than the fresh water in the tunnel and tasted salty as she pushed her head above the surface gasping for breath.

Emily surfaced right beside the boat, which had landed right side up but was empty. She grabbed the side of the craft, grateful for its presence as she breathed deeply, the tightness in her chest slowly subsiding. She had six or seven gold necklaces around her neck and the weight pulled her down. Holding onto the side of the boat Emily looked around at a scene of chaos and devastation. All of them had returned to the surface and were looking in horror at a rocky outcrop, dark against the frothy white water.

Maggie lay crumpled on its point, her battered body bleeding profusely into the water that rose and fell around her. Limbs jutted out awkwardly and raw flesh exposed bones. She wasn't moving, wasn't breathing, life pouring from her with every surge of the waves which washed up and covered her. Emily realized that even if her mother was alive, there wasn't the medical technology needed to save her anywhere around, even if they got her back to the ship.

As if to put an end to any such thought, a huge wave washed over the rocks and dragged her body off the pinnacle. Emily turned away, unable to watch. Her lungs burned from lack of oxygen. Now, added to that was a stabbing pain in her heart. She had just met Maggie, her real mother, and there were so many more questions she had wanted to ask. There was so much more about her mother's life she wanted to know, but never would. What was her favorite color, where did she like to go on vacation, and what was her favorite song?

Numbly, the thirteen women began swimming for the boat. The treasure lay scattered on the ocean floor. Most had cuts and bruises from the fall, but other than Maggie, no one was seriously hurt. They clambered aboard, exhausted, and frightened, tipping the narrowboat wildly from side to side as the rest of the soggy women pushed themselves and whatever jewels they were wearing out of the water and into the boat. They sat staring at the rock, now cleaned of blood, where Maggie had died.

Emily didn't know what to do with the upwelling of emotion that washed through her, so she pulled off the necklaces she wore around her neck and tossed them into the boat, took a deep breath, and dove to the bottom, picking up objects and bringing them to the surface, handing them to the women in the boat. Others joined her and for an hour they went up and down until they had retrieved everything and loaded it into the boat. The sun was beginning to drop to the horizon when Emily finally heaved herself up, with Mary's help, into the boat.

Emily surveyed the crew in the boat as they set out to find the ship. The boat had never had oars, so the women leaned over the sides and paddled with their arms. It was slow progress, and the sun was set, the sky a fiery reddish-orange, when they finally paddled their way back to the anchored ship. The waterfall had dumped them out on the other side of the island. Maggie's body now lay there as if sleeping on the beach. It was as fitting a grave as anyone could think of and so they left her there, Bedalia would look over her. They loaded the recovered gold and jewels into the ship and tied the long narrow boat to its side. Stars filled the night sky as they sat around the wooden table in the galley and took stock of the day. Maggie's death overshadowed the excitement of finding the treasure. Emily felt a profound sadness, as she had when her father died, like the one thing that kept you safely anchored to the ground was suddenly gone. She sat morosely at the end of the table, eyes down, tears welling up.

"We should go back to where her body is and hold a memorial service."

"No!" barked Bedalia, startling everyone. "Hornigold might already know where this island is, he won't be fooled for long by Mary's ruse, and if he's lucky he can find the entrance to the cave, though I doubt he can guess the password. Let's not give him another clue and another entrance. Besides," she lifted her eyebrows and winked, "I will watch over Maggie and you all might want to come back for more."

The talk around the table rose and fell like the waves, moving from the highs of the ride in the little narrowboat out the tunnel over the waterfall and into the ocean, to the lows of the shock and horror of seeing Maggie's battered body splayed across the rock. They laughed with amazement that they had hummed their way past the prodigious snake and spoke in awe of the pile of gold and jewels they had seen, most of which remained hidden in the cave.

"It's all ours, isn't it?" Mary asked,

"Yes, it is," said Bedalia.

"Bedalia - what will happen to Maggie?" Emily asked. Tears stung her eyes.

"Interesting question. Only time will tell."

Emily found that a maddeningly vague answer and it hinted at something that had been worrying her. Now that they had all met, might history be forever changed? Could she go back to her time, did she even exist then?

"It doesn't change history for any of the rest of us, right?"

"The treasure will have some effect."

Each contemplated what impact having the gold might have on her own life. Emily had no idea what the necklaces and cups she had collected were worth. The thing she would bring back that meant the most was meeting her birth mother.

"So, what's next? I mean, we've found the treasure, which was the whole point wasn't it? So, when do we go back?" Emily was suddenly anxious to return to the mother she knew, who must have given up hope that she'd ever see her daughter again.

The women looked around the room, eyes searching for an answer. Most eventually settled on Mary and Bedalia who had moved to stand directly behind her. Mary looked tired, incredibly young, and suddenly unsure of herself.

"I don't know. It all seems so sudden..." Her voice trailed

off.

"We must return to the point we began," Bedalia said firmly, "near Bermuda."

"Why Bermuda?" Winnie asked.

"It is a mystical place where many things amazing and not easily understood can happen."

Emily and Izzie nodded in agreement. The correct headings were determined by Maddie and the cycle of watches was re-established. The ship was heading towards Bermuda, the treacherous seas around the island, and the promise of going home. Emily thought about the baby. It was at least a week older now, and in little snippets was gaining a stronger hold on her thoughts. The idea of keeping the baby seemed more rational now in this environment, surrounded by women who had made a different decision and regretted it. Would that same idea seem so ordinary when she was back in her own time, living at home and working at her job? She could undo the pregnancy, but could she un-do what had changed in her heart?

CHAPTER TWENTY-FOUR

EMILY

The ship softly rocked Emily's hammock from side to side. It was becoming so familiar that she wondered if she would ever be able to sleep on dry land again. She remembered a hamster she had as a kid. It went around in its wheel all night, endlessly going around in a squeaky, rhythmic circle. It kept her up until one night she didn't hear it anymore. It wasn't that the hamster wasn't going around, but her brain had filtered it out. When the hamster died and the sound stopped, she couldn't sleep, the quiet was too deafening. The hammock cradled her body and the whoosh, whoosh sound of the water against the hull of the ship made her feel like a fetus in the womb of *The Maryann.*

A familiar scent drifted past Emily as she rocked in her nest, acrid, distinct, like a skunk. What would smell like a skunk in a place far from any real skunks, she wondered, and as she searched her memory, she heard a faint sound. It was a creaking sound, distinct from all the creaking that an old wooden ship did as a matter of course lumbering through the uneven waters of the Caribbean Sea.

Emily held her breath to better hear the sound. It was moving in the darkness. Another ghost perhaps? The sound altered to a soft clanging sound. In the blackness, she couldn't see her relatives sleeping in their hammocks. Up on deck one or two of her ancestors were keeping watch. They would have sounded the alarm if intruders had boarded the ship. All had been quiet from the deck, perhaps the sounds had been the usual ringing in her ears.

She shifted in her hammock and two of the gold charms softly jangled around her neck. There! That was the sound. It wasn't so much a lack of trust that drove them each to wear the necklaces as it was a fear that they would somehow vanish. The cups and larger items they had been able to recover from the sea bottom after falling filled trunks in the hold. Emily kept her trunk directly below her hammock so she could use it as a stepping block. The group had decided to give her Maggie's share and that too was in the wooden trunk. Maggie's hammock was empty. Emily couldn't see it, but she could feel its presence.

Emily heard the sound again, it was real, and was getting closer. It was a creaking followed by the sound of metal clanking together. In her mind's eye, Emily traveled around the interior of the hold, seeking a source for the sound, yet she kept coming back to the trunks, full of gold and jewels. Someone was opening the trunks and stealing their treasure. Who would do that?

182

Could Mary be so unwilling to share after all the help her descendants had given her, she would sneak around in the dark and take back what they had brought out. The acrid smell again passed Emily, whoever was riffling through the trunks, was near her. Her muscles froze; Mary had never had such an unwashed odor to her. The smell was like a sweaty gym locker, a male smell. Unless Hornigold had found them again the only man on board was Henry.

Uncle Henry, could he be more like his brother than not? Emily barely breathed. How dangerous was Henry? All along he had made himself out to be weak, injured, keeping in the background. Was that a complete act, and all the while he was waiting for this moment to steal the treasure from them?

If he was a pirate, then he might be extremely dangerous, she reasoned, and so she didn't move, did not confront him. In the morning she would confirm whether anything was missing.

Emily woke to a commotion. Things were missing out of half the trunks.

"Did anyone see that gold cup with the rubies? It's missing from my things," Winnie said as she rummaged through her trunk.

Emily remained quiet. If Blackbeard's brother was also a pirate, how dangerous was he? Her heart rate began to climb, pounding in her ears, a vision of the ship sailing on its own with a dead crew taking over her thoughts. She sat up with courage she had never felt before and swung out of her hammock.

Henry was alone in the galley, cooking porridge for breakfast.

"Sleep well, Henry?"

"Yeah," He didn't look up.

"Henry, tell me again why you're here and not safely back in jolly old England with your Mum?"

Her sarcastic tone was hard to miss, though she suspected he did.

"Just came to help my little brother."

"How many brothers and sisters are there?"

"Three boys, I'm the middle," he returned to stirring the thick, pasty-looking porridge.

"So, if Blackbeard is the youngest and you're the middle, who's the oldest?"

"Lord Beadington."

"Beadington? I thought your last name was Teach."

"Mum's family name is Teach. Dad's is Beadington. Eddy and Father didn't get along so when Father shipped him off to the navy, he started using Mum's family name."

Emily poured herself a cup of hot water and pulled open the metal tin of dried leaves.

"So, your name is Henry, Blackbeard's name is Edward, and your eldest brother is Lord Beadington.

She stirred the leaves.

"If Teddy is a Lord, I'm assuming that means something important, parliament maybe, and Ed was sent to the navy, what are you?"

The question struck him as hard as a pointed metal spear. His face squinted as if he'd sucked on a lemon. He shook it off and resumed stirring.

"I take care of the estate. It's a large house with thousands of acres, takes quite a lot."

He sat down heavily on a wooden bench and rubbed his leg. "Hurt this when a horse kicked me."

The man in front of her was changing from a sailor, even a pirate, into a country gentleman farmer. Layers of salt and grime covered the China and cashmere of wealth. Uncle Henry was no more a seasoned pirate than Emily and her grandmothers were. Yet she was sure it was him she had heard stealing Blackbeard's treasure from their trunks.

"Where did you learn to cook?" she asked him.

"Oh, we had to let the cook go when money got tight, and mother can't cook, shouldn't cook. I don't think she's quite right in the head anymore, and hearing that Eddy was causing trouble hit her hard."

Emily envisioned a small, white-haired little lady sitting in a brocade chair in a large drafty room. It put the wooden chair Mary had found in the tower into context. Blackbeard had been raised in elegant style. His older brother was a lord in parliament, and he was a notorious pirate. Then there was Henry, quiet, unassuming Henry, who stayed home to take care of the family estate and his mother. Following Blackbeard to the Caribbean, to help his wayward little brother was a selfish bid to grab some of the glory and adventure. He didn't even have the decency to look guilty.

"You asked me not to tell anyone you were our uncle, but I can't keep that secret anymore."

Henry slowly nodded his head. "I guess it's time to tell Mary."

"I'll let you do that but do it quickly." Emily rose and began to climb the stairs to the deck. She paused and looked back over her shoulder, "and put the stuff you stole back please." She turned and continued up the steps without looking back to see if his face registered surprise.

CHAPTER TWENTY-FIVE

EMILY

Maggie was on Emily's mind. Ever since her death and their quick departure from the island, there were questions. Questions about what would happen to Maggie and how her death could even have happened, since in this time, 1719, she hadn't been born.

Emily reached the deck to see the first hint of the morning on the horizon, a lightening of the inky blackness. By dawn most of the women were sitting in a large circle, organized in chronological order, Emily sitting between Mary and Izzie, her biological grandmother. She realized with a wave of guilt that she hadn't thought much about her adopted family the entire time she'd been on this ship, however long that had been. Surrounded by her biological family, this circle of women across multiple generations, Emily placed her hand on her still flat abdomen trying to connect with the child growing silently inside her. She saw a flash of the baby girl lying in her crib with Mark and Emily looking down as doting parents.

She flushed at the thought of a future with Mark. Beyond the one night together and the brief time she spent telling him about the baby they had not spent any time together. What sort of husband or father would he be? Was she in love with him or could she fall in love with him? In her dream, they were already a family.

Time rushed forward and back, hard to pin down. The strangeness of the time warp that enveloped the whole ship and crew made Emily begin to wonder if Maggie could somehow come back – as she was when she came on board the ship. Emily convinced herself she could see a shadow of Maggie sitting where her trunk of belongings sat. She was wearing her yellow sundress with black buttons and crisp black piping along the edges. Her hair was pulled back, not blown around as all their hair had been on board. If Maggie was here with them, then what was time if it was so fluid as to allow all these generations to sit in a circle and mourn one of them? When Emily returned to her time, which she held on to the belief she would, would time have passed equally to the time on board, or would it be a blink of an eye and no one would have known she was gone? Would she even remember?

Mary suggested that everyone say something they would remember about Maggie. Emily went first.

"Maggie was, is, my mother, and I'm proud to be her daughter. We were just getting to know each other when…" she paused, a sob stuck in her throat. "I would have liked more time, but I do know she was a loving person, and I will miss her."

Tears were visible sliding down cheeks around the circle, shining in the early morning light. They sat quietly for a moment, the ship rocking gently on a calm sea. Ann's call from the crow's nest broke the spell.

"Ship ahoy on the leeward side to stern, we've got company!" she bellowed.

Henry, Mary, and Emily dashed across the deck and up the stairs as fast as they could to the wheel, where Emily had left the spyglass. Henry raised it to his eye and peered through it. After a tense moment, he confirmed the sighting.

"Hornigold."

"Damn!" said Emily and the rest of the group scrambled to their feet, rushing to the ship's side to see what was happening. Off in the distance, a ship in full sail was heading for them, the sun flashing on the white sails that billowed out in the wind.

"I thought we'd lost him," said Izzie. Mary took the spyglass from Henry and peered through it.

"Well, we found him again."

"Ladies," Bedalia called out to the crew, "we need all the sails trimmed as tightly as we can, we need speed," and with the precision of a drill team they all turned on their heels and began a synchronized effort to trim the sails. Mary stayed with Henry and Bedalia while Emily took off at a run, eager to channel her energy into something useful. But she didn't head for the sails.

"Where are you going?" Mary called after her.

"To hoist Blackbeard's flag," she replied and dashed down the steps to the galley. The flag was not perfect but was close enough and would have to do. Winnie had spent countless hours on the flag, piecing together pieces of cloth she found on the ship. The skeleton and spear were identical to the drawing, but the heart was more finely shaped. Winnie had been unable to bring herself to reproduce the crudely made heart that Blackbeard had flown.

When Emily reappeared with the flag, she handed it to Izzie who was closest to her as she climbed out of the hold and Izzie quickly tied it to a rope and pulled it up to the top of the mast. Blackbeard's colors were flying again, blowing in the wind over the deck below. The wind napped it crisply from side to side as if testing to see if it was sturdy enough.

"I'm not sure why," Emily said, looking up at the whipping pirate flag, "but it seems the right thing to do."

Henry shook his head in disagreement. "It puts us in league with the devil." He stomped off to see about cannons.

Despite setting the sails perfectly, the Dutch Flaut was a lumbering barge of a ship and was just not fast enough to outrun Hornigold's sloop. It felt to Emily like she was in a huge traffic jam with an important meeting coming up, powerless to make things move and her chest feeling squeezed by the stress.

Tension across the ship rose as the realization settled in that an actual pirate ship was hunting them, this wasn't a game. Bedalia stepped forward, like she had waited for this very moment, and assumed command of the ship, ordering everyone to arm themselves. She then sent ten of the women below deck to find anything heavy that could be used as a weapon.

They had instructions to collect what they could and then to come back to the top deck and hide in the captain's quarters. That left four women on deck, five counting Bedalia. They were prepared for the first onslaught of pirates from Hornigold's ship.

Mary turned to Bedalia, putting her hands on the woman's forearm, and said a quiet "thank you" before she ran off to help pry the cover off the large wooden box on deck and pull the glistening steel and silver swords out of its depths. Mary joined Emily and examined the cutlass she was holding, swinging it back and forth to regain the feel of its heft and weight.

"When we played around with these those first days, I didn't think we'd have to use them. I'm afraid we are going to be outclassed in a fight with pirates who use these cutlasses every day. Does Bedalia have any magic that could help us fight better?" Emily asked Mary.

"Do you think we'll have to fight?" Mary asked in a stage whisper, Emily nodded yes. The easy banter of the past week was gone. The four women stood swinging cutlass blades in the air, their eyes glued to the ship advancing so close to them that at any moment grappling hooks would start flying over the railing, connecting the two ships again. The last time that happened resulted in kidnapping, what would happen this time? Did Hornigold know they had found the treasure? Or was he still looking for the map? Emily knew that this time their encounter with Hornigold wouldn't end with someone left on an island to die. This time would end with bloody bodies and a broken ship.

Izzie came over to stand beside her granddaughter.

"Mary, these women can't fight a real pirate! We were play-acting when we learned to handle the cutlass, no one thought it was for real. We'll be slaughtered!"

Emily thought of her baby and her mother, Sydney. She may be adopted, but Sydney had been there for her. Emily desperately wanted to tell her about the baby.

"They say your life flashes before your eyes when you are in real danger, but all I'm seeing is the life of my child."

Izzie put her arm around her granddaughter's shoulder. Mary turned to look at Emily.

"You are carrying a child? Why haven't you said anything?"

"I didn't want anyone to know. I'm not exactly proud of it, like all of you it wasn't a planned baby. I'm...I'm not sure I'm going to keep it." Mary shook her head.

"You're talking nonsense. You should not fight this fight. Protect your child."

"You will need every woman to fight Mary, I'll be careful," Emily assured her.

CHAPTER TWENTY-SIX

EMILY

Izzie stayed close to Emily, mothering her in the absence of Maggie.

My grandmother, Emily thought, and her mind drifted to her adopted mother and instantly flooded with guilt. She doesn't know where I am, and if something happens, she wouldn't know what had become of me.

There was no way to get a message to her, to thank her, and tell her she loved her. In that space where life and death seemed intertwined, Emily realized that having known her biological mother didn't change the relationship she had with her adopted mother, hadn't lessened it as she feared it would. It had strengthened it.

She had moved from anger at learning she was adopted to seeing the woman who had raised her as her own, cared for her when she was sick, and seen her through all the terrible teenage years as her real mother. She had to survive this somehow for these two women, who were the reason she was who she was.

Her thoughts cut short when the first grappling hook landed on the railing and dug in, digging a trench in the well-polished wood. *The Maryann* groaned at the attack.

"Are you ready?" Izzie asked Emily. Emily nodded yes, whatever was going to happen it was going to happen now. They turned to stand side by side, cutlasses out and ready for the first two pirates to come swinging onto the deck. The men landed with a sickening thud on the deck, but quickly regained their balance, their blades ready for attack. They looked every bit the part of a ragged pirate. Each wore a red cotton shirt, torn and repaired endless times. Black pants, bare feet, and bandanas holding back greasy, long hair. The pirates laughed when they saw the four women, "This will be easy!"

The fighting began as more pirates swung over from the sloop and landed on the clean deck. *The Maryann*, once derelict, now gleamed, even as blades dug into her wood, chipping the railings. Steel clanged against steel, wood splinters flew whenever a blade missed its mark and hit the railing or the mast. Dancing back and forth in a fight with one of the pirates, a sharp reverberation raced through Emily's arm whenever her blade met the pirate's blade, causing her hand to bounce back. More pirates poured over the railing onto the deck, which was getting slippery with blood and wood splinters.

Izzie thrust a blade into her opponent's chest, the pirate falling back and crumpling.

"When will you decide whether to keep the child?" she asked Emily before turning again to duel the next pirate who appeared, ready to take his comrade's place.

"This is hardly the time or place to talk about it." She swung her blade through the air with two hands and hit her opponent with the broad side of the blade against his head so hard he fell unconscious on the spot. The vibration traveled up her arms and through her ears.

"It is a wholly appropriate time. You are risking the life of an unborn child in this fight, without having given thought to whether it will remain unborn, now help me dump this guy overboard." Emily took the slumped pirate by one arm and helped wrestle him over the railing.

"Really Izzie, isn't all this strange enough without laying that guilt on me?"

"Oh Em, I'm not trying to lay guilt, it's just that I don't want you to repeat all the mistakes we've made," she held her granddaughter's shoulders, careful not to cut her with the cutlass, and looked at her straight in the eyes.

"You are our only hope to break the curse."

"Watch out!" Emily called out, as a blade swung close to Izzie's head. Izzie ducked and they rejoined the fight.

Hornigold alone remained on his ship watching the battle progress. When his crew was all aboard *The Maryann,* he grabbed a rope from the yardarm and swung across himself.

Emily watched as he flew.

That pompous ass, she thought, he waited to join the fight to allow his men the chance to fight and defeat us before getting his own hands dirty. Well, we've got a surprise for him; his men are falling faster than we are. Indeed, several men lay prostrate on the ground, blood oozing from wounds, while none of the four women were injured.

Hornigold landed on the deck and looked around for Mary. He raised his sword to swing at her and Mary swirled in place and sliced at him on his thighs.

"You cur!" he shouted, wincing at the slashes in his pants and flesh.

"I should not have trusted a woman. You deceived me with your directions, but not for long."

"You were easily deceived," Mary taunted him. "We found the cave, and it is empty. The legend is just a tale drunkards tell each other." Emily was surprised at how easily Mary lied.

"False words!" Hornigold exclaimed. "I know Blackbeard would not have moved the treasure and I've verified the story of Captain Morgan with others. It should be my treasure!"

"If it existed, it would not be your treasure, it is Blackbeard's treasure and the treasure of his family," Mary replied. "It is our right to claim."

"Ha, your ship is small and your crew even smaller. Once we've dispatched you, we will search this vessel and find whatever treasure you stole. I've no doubt you will fight with courage, but you are nothing but women -masquerading as pirates, fighting a band of tested brethren of the code."

He swung his blade at Mary, and she swung hers in return. Ann came over to help and the two battled Hornigold.

"I'm sorry I got you into this mess Ann," Mary said over her shoulder.

"You're sorry I was born," Ann countered, swinging her blade, and narrowly missing the pirate's arm.

"You're right, I was," confessed Mary as she swung her blade at a new pirate to join the battle, "but not now, I see my mistake and I'd like to spend more time with you if that is possible."

She swung around so that they now had Hornigold between them. "What in blazes are you talking about?" Hornigold shouted.

"It's none of your bloody business!" Ann yelled back.

Turning, Ann saw five of the pirates heading their way.

"Ladies" she called out, "we need some more help!" The rest of the women poured out of the Captain's Quarters armed with swords and anything heavy they could carry. They raced up the stairs to the ship's wheel and leaning over the railing that looked down on the deck dropped the frying pans, ballast rocks, and small casks onto the heads of the unsuspecting pirates, knocking most to the ground unconscious. After stepping back to allow the debris to hit the pirates Emily, Izzie, Mary, and Ann rushed over to take on the few that made it through the fusillade.

More pirates swarmed over from the sloop. Hornigold had used the same trick, hiding some of his crew as reserves.

The women on the wheel deck were lightly armed and unprepared for the fight that came to them. Blades were swinging and people were shouting. In a quick turn, the crew of *The Maryann* Hornigold's men outnumbered them. In short order, Sarah and Winnie were laying on the deck and Emily couldn't tell if they were dead or not. Other women looked injured as well, although Emily couldn't tell who they were. Caroline was moving carefully among the wounded women, pulling them off to the side where she could perform some first aid and assess their situation when, with a banging crash, a cannonball hit the side of *The Maryann* and a shudder traveled through the ship.

CHAPTER TWENTY-SEVEN

EMILY

Mary's eyes flew wide open.

"What was that?" she screamed. Before Emily could decide where the blast had originated from, a second cannonball came careening across and hit the mainmast, thick wood splinters flying everywhere.

With an eerie creaking sound, the mainmast began leaning to starboard, and after hanging awkwardly for a moment slowly fell toward the deck. The last ten feet of the mast crashed down, flattening the ship's wheel, and partially caving in the roof of the Captain's Quarters. Women and pirates flew in all directions as they ran to get out of the way of the mast itself and the sails and ropes that came down with it.

Izzie fought her way out from under a huge sail by slicing her way through the material with a blade.

"Emily where are you?" she yelled.

"Under here," came Emily's voice, muffled by the yards of

canvas piled on top of her.

"Hold still." The cutlass sliced the sail close enough to draw blood. She stuck an arm out of the hole her grandmother had created and pushed the material back to free herself of the tangled mess.

"Thanks."

"Don't mention it. We have more company."

At the crash of the first cannonball, the pirates and the women had stopped fighting, blades frozen in midair. As one, they turned their heads to look where the cannonball had come from and saw a large warship sitting off the other side of *The Maryann* and moving closer.

Hornigold put down his blade and stood beside Mary, Izzie, and Emily, staring at the warship on the starboard side of *The Maryann* creating a sandwich with the sloop on one side and the Dutch Fleut in the middle.

"Maynard!" Hornigold spat out, "that's the bastard that killed Blackbeard."

Emily watched the approaching warship with horror, the nightmare with Hornigold's ship paling in comparison to this new threat. Hornigold had simply wanted the treasure, but Maynard wanted pirates, and in his eyes, they were all pirates. They were flying Blackbeard's Jolly Roger. What had seemed like a promising idea now seemed foolish. It had drawn the interest of those who hunted and killed pirates.

Emily doubted that Captain Maynard would see them

fighting the pirates and believe them to be on his side. She felt her heart pounding, pushing blood through her body in preparation for the impending need and threatening to blow out her ears. Looking around she saw her family, her grandmothers and great grandmothers with blood flushing their faces red, anticipating the new battle ahead.

Where was Henry? Their ship, *The Maryann*, mortally wounded, with its mast broken into many pieces, listed to port. Damage to the ship felt like damage to them. The hours spent repairing the ship and bringing her to the glory that she had been new, were hours during which the women had talked, compared lives, shared secrets, and wondered aloud at the mysterious way they came together.

They didn't have the skills or the materials to repair the damage the ship now sustained, making any type of escape impossible. How would they return to their lives if the ship sank, unable to return to the Bermuda waters? Was Bedalia's magic strong enough to overcome this setback? Were they now all truly dead?

Emily looked around for Bedalia. She had been solidly in charge, giving orders right up to the point of the first grappling hook. With that, she had vanished. Emily realized they were on their own. Henry was still absent.

"Mary, how many cannons do we have onboard?" Emily shouted over the din. Emily had not thought to look for cannons during their time onboard. Never in her wildest imagination did she dream they would need to fire off such a primitive weapon.

"Four," came Henry's strong voice, "none of which will likely fire." So that was where he had gone, to count the number of cannons?

"How many cannons do you think Maynard has?" Mary asked. Henry hesitated only a moment,

"Ship that size, probably twenty cannons," he guessed. Twenty cannons against four, we're doomed Emily moaned, but why is he firing at us?

More grappling hooks swung through the air and grabbed the starboard railing, splinters of wood flying. The three ships were connected, *The Maryann* trapped between the two.

Unlike Hornigold, Maynard was in the first group of sailors to swing over and land on the jumbled deck of *The Maryann*. The loss of the mainmast had caused ropes and sailcloth to fall across the deck, masking what was beneath and making footing difficult. Maynard spotted Hornigold immediately and pulled his sword out of its sheath as he walked slowly towards the old pirate.

"Captain Hornigold, I presume?" Maynard asked.

"You know damn well who I am," challenged Hornigold. "We're on the same side, I hunt pirates too. I caught this band of petticoat buccaneers and plan to return them to Bermuda and present them to the governor."

"I should advise you, Captain Hornigold," Maynard raised his sword a bit higher, "that I have information to the contrary, and it is you I am hunting. I have no information that this ship of

202

women poses a threat. The fact that you are fighting them is of no consequence. You, on the other hand, are a concern to the people of Virginia."

"I'm a gentleman farmer of the Bahamas Islands. I work with The Honorable Woodes Rogers and serve at his pleasure."

"I'm afraid you are very wrong on that point sir," Maynard informed him, "for it is Mr. Woodes Rogers that informed us of your deceit and where we might find you. You may surrender peacefully which might help your cause in the Pirate's Court, though I very much doubt it."

As Emily watched, Hornigold's face grew red and angry-looking. The veins in his neck bulged out and his hand gripped his cutlass so tightly she could see them turn white. He took a step back and pointed his blade at Maynard, "I do not surrender to anyone!"

The battle began anew; the sounds of sword on sword rang out. It was chaos, every man and woman for themselves.

"Fighting sir will only afford you the same fate as your friend Blackbeard, a violent death and the loss of your head," Maynard called out.

Emily and Izzie were again fighting side by side. It was hard to know who to fight and their new opponents were better armed and skilled than their previous ones. As they fought, they periodically stepped on an unconscious pirate buried under the sails. Any that revived and managed to work their way out from under the canvas were momentarily confused as to which side they were now on and started fighting with anyone nearby.

Emily's arms were tired. She had just dropped her arms to rest when a soldier appeared in front of her.

"Sorry fella," she cried and swung her blade forcefully and with precision, slicing his arm off. Blood poured out of the wound, causing Emily to wince at the sight and gag as bile moved into her throat. She looked at her cutlass in wonder, as if the blade had acted alone. Izzie parried over towards her, battling a ragged-looking soldier that couldn't have been more than fifteen years old.

"Nice swing," she called out to Emily, "would you help me with this one?"

"Sure, let's move him towards the railing and flip him over, I'm getting tired of hurting people." Izzie nodded yes and the two combined forces to push the young soldier up against the railing, then while Izzie kept his blade busy Emily reached down, grabbed his legs, and flipped him back over the railing.

"Agghhh," he cried when he hit the water, "I can't swim, help!"

"Can't swim? Can you imagine that makes his living on the water and he can't swim? You'd think that would be the first thing he'd learn how to do. Fighting skills aren't much use if getting washed over and drowning is the biggest worry." Emily looked around at the action on the deck of *The Maryann*.

"We're winning!" she called out.

"Emily, have you decided whether I'm going to be a great-grandmother? Are you going to break the curse?" Izzie asked.

"You keep talking of a curse, what curse?" Emily asked.

"The curse of giving up your child, of being an orphan," Izzie answered bitterly, "The curse we've all lived with, even you."

"This is still not a good time to talk about that, don't you think?" Emily answered.

"It is a terrific time to talk about it. Before I have a sword run through me, I want to know," her great-grandmother said. Emily sighed.

"I can't imagine not having this baby. After meeting Maggie, you, and all the others, I'll have more than enough help raising the baby. I don't know how my adoptive mother will take it, or all this. It is just her and me since Dad died. All this may devastate her, she'll be mad at me, that's for sure, but whether she and I can get past that is the big question."

Izzie wrapped her granddaughter in a huge bear hug. "I'm proud of you for making a decision none of the women on this ship were brave enough to make. Somehow, we will be here to help you make that decision a successful one, and I can't wait to meet my great-granddaughter."

Emily laughed, "So you think it is a girl as well?"

"Of course, it's a girl, look around you, what else could it be?"

Emily watched the fighting between Hornigold and Maynard, soldiers, pirates, and women all fighting each other.

"Why are we in the middle of this fight?" she wondered aloud, "this is between soldiers and pirates, not us."

"Ladies!" she called out, "fall back!" Mary looked over from her position on the railing and nodded.

"This isn't our fight!" Emily called out. Slowly and quietly the women drew back into the shattered remains of the Captain's Quarters, leaving the pirates and soldiers to fight each other. The interior of the cabin was in total disarray from the mast which had smashed through the wheel deck above. The women pushed aside all the broken furniture and glass. When they were all there, Emily closed the door and did a quick count, finding only twelve women.

"We're missing someone, who isn't here?"

Winnie's voice came from the corner of the room, "I don't see Sophia."

"We'll have to find her, but this isn't our battle, let's let the warship and Hornigold battle it out. Maynard doesn't appear to be interested in us, so let's not give him a reason to get interested."

"What happens if Hornigold wins?" Mary asked.

"Then we'll pick up where we left off, but there will be fewer pirates and we'll be better rested and able to fight stronger."

Emily and Izzie searched the deck for Sophia. Once on the deck, Emily could see Sophia's leg sticking out from under the sailcloth that had fallen with the mast. She pointed this out to Izzie and dodging fighting pirates and soldiers, the two moved carefully over to the leg and pulled the sailcloth away. Sophia was barely breathing, her head looked bashed in, from the mast, Emily thought.

"Do you think we can move her?" Emily asked.

"I don't think we have a choice; we need to get her to the Captain's Quarters so Caroline can treat her." Emily nodded and moving together they slid Sophia towards them and gently picked her up. The deck of the ship was moving back and forth in the waves, which made walking on the slippery surface difficult. It felt like forever to Emily before they reached the doors to the Captain's Quarters and brought Sophia inside. They lay her on the cushioned window seat and stepped back to let Caroline treat her wounds.

It seemed to Emily that as soon as she had laid Sophia down on the cushion that all sound stopped. Looking around she realized it had stopped, a strange quiet had settled over the ship. She backed out of the room to check on the fighting, knowing at some point one side would win and the women would have to either fight or figure out what to do with a sinking ship. Stepping out of the Captain's Quarters she felt a change in the air and turned to see a sight that defied logic even in the twisted reality within which their whole adventure had been staged.

A figure Emily had never expected to see stood on the broken mast, surveying the scene below him. His vast black beard was braided and looped up over his ears on both sides of his head, ready for battle.

Smoke drifted up from wicks stuck in the braids, creating a halo of white smoke around his head. He wore a red coat, black britches, and leather boots.

Blackbeard was back.

CHAPTER TWENTY-EIGHT

EMILY

Captain Maynard saw Blackbeard at the same time Emily did. He stumbled backward missing a well-placed jab by Hornigold.

"You," he spluttered at Blackbeard, "you're dead, I...I killed you myself!"

Blackbeard turned to face Maynard and Hornigold. Hornigold looked dumbfounded, his slacken jaw hanging open. Henry came up from below deck, where he had retreated once the real fighting had started, and stood next to Emily at the door of the Captain's Quarters.

"Death itself is relative," Blackbeard replied calmly but with a hint of menace that was impossible to miss.

"And these fine people," he pointed towards the Captain's Quarters where Henry and all the women were now watching through the doorway, "are my family, my relatives."

Maynard and Hornigold looked from Blackbeard to the women.

"Well," Mary said, "small point of correction. We are all relatives; however, Henry is just hired help."

Henry turned to face her and took her hands in his.

"Mary," he said, "I'm your brother-in-law. Ed is, or was, my little brother." Mary's eyes widened in surprise.

"You didn't tell her!" Emily yelled. Henry shrugged and looked away.

Blackbeard pulled his sword out of the scabbard hanging at his hip.

"Now, get on your little boats and sail away before any of my deceased pirate friends come and help you,"

Maynard's crew wasted no time responding and did not wait for an order. As a group, they rushed to the starboard side and scrambled over to the warship. Maynard kept his sword raised as he backed over to the rail, never letting Blackbeard out of his sight. With one swift movement, he sprung to the railing and leaped the distance to his ship. Axes began cutting the ropes of the grappling hooks and with haste, the ship moved away from *The Maryann.*

Blackbeard raised his scabbard and pointed it at Hornigold.

"That goes for you too," indicating with the tip of his blade that Hornigold should get on his ship. "Kindly leave my family and my treasure alone."

Hornigold slowly sheathed his blade and touched the brim of his hat in a nod to Blackbeard. With that, he walked to the port side railing and climbed over to the sloop. His remaining crew followed silently, not wishing more dead pirates to appear and bring untold bad luck.

The women of *The Maryann* stood silently in the presence of the feared pirate and their grandsire. Blackbeard remained on the mast, silently looking at each of them.

Henry, it's good to see you. How's Mum?"

"Well, she won't be happy to hear you're dead, but she will like hearing she as all these new relatives."

Blackbeard nodded and turned his attention to the women.

"You've done well in your search for the treasure. But then you are all my daughters, except you Mary," he nodded in her direction," and I would expect nothing less from the daughters of Blackbeard, the notorious Pirate!" He held his sword in the air in salute to himself.

"Did you come to our aid?" Mary asked.

"I may have caused a storm or two," he replied and winked. Emily thought his face looked almost kindly when he smiled.

"Then thank you, sir," Mary said. "You've given a legacy to this family that cannot be matched by others."

"Aye, that I've done," he replied.

With a shudder *The Maryann* heaved to the port side, having taken in water through the cannonball holes. Emily knew it was only a matter of time before the ship sank, and not much time at that. The dinghy they rode out of the cave was still tied to the starboard side. It would hold them all without any of the treasure.

Would they all die like Maggie?

"We lost my mother because of all this," she said.

Blackbeard took his hat off and held it over his heart.

"Aye, you did. But one of the rewards of being dead and having Bedalia to help is that things like that could change."

"Will they change? Will Maggie be okay?"

"Perhaps." It wasn't all she had hoped for but maybe Maggie would still be there in her own time.

"What will happen to us?" Someone asked.

Blackbeard looked at the group. Emily thought that he didn't seem to be in any hurry despite their sinking ship. "Madeline, what is our bearing?"
Maddie's voice faltered when she tried to speak.

"We should have reached the Bermuda waters, sir, based on last night's readings."

"Then it must be time. Bedalia!" He bellowed with a voice that was around and inside them at the same time.

With a flash of light, Bedalia was standing next to him. The women gasped and took a step back. Bedalia had been a mysterious person from the beginning when each woman met her in the tea shop.

Now she looked angelic. Her eyes glowed like the night on the beach of the little hour-glass island, the beach she had died on.

Emily was sure now that they had talked that night and that Bedalia was an angel. Did angels love pirates? This one does, and because of her love, she had enabled a family of women to meet and establish the bonds that families need to survive.

Emily had found a mother she had never known and embraced a daughter that was yet only a flicker of life.

"Are we done?" Blackbeard asked her.

"We are done,"

"Mary, my key please," Blackbeard extended out an open palm. With visible reluctance, she removed it from around her neck and placed it on his hand. His big fingers closed around the key and Emily felt the familiar sensation of blackness pushing the air out of her lungs. She reached out for Izzie's hand, but couldn't find it, nothing but space surrounded her.

CHAPTER TWENTY-NINE

EMILY

Gusts of salty wind brushed Emily's face as she sat meditating on the worn wooden bench, blowing the purple silk scarf she wore around her neck. She opened her eyes and blinked. The seashore was quiet, the morning rain kept most beachgoers away; the air was clear and the sky a crisp blue. The sounds of the waves almost drowned out the gentle snoring of the blonde-haired man sitting next to her. Mark had never been into meditation but didn't mind a good nap when he got the chance.

Emily remembered the day, twelve years ago, she had returned from *The Maryann* to find herself standing on the sidewalk in front of a trendy women's dress shop. There was no sign of a tea shop or an old sailing ship. It had taken a few minutes for her to get her bearings, while shoppers gave her wide birth.

'I must look a fright,' she thought remembering that she hadn't changed out of the tunic and capris that she had been wearing as she had been fighting for her life with a cutlass against pirates and soldiers on a ship that was sinking.

'I'd avoid getting near me too.' She looked down at her clothes and to her surprise saw only khaki pants and a pale blue button-down shirt. How could that be? Was it all a dream or hallucination?

'None of it happened. I wonder how long I've been standing here like a dope.'

Then she reached into her pocket and found the necklace, rings, and coins and felt the gold bracelet on her wrist. Some of the treasure had made it back with her, it had happened, and she was back, she was alive.

She remembered it all, her mother Maggie, Mary, all the grandmothers between Ann and Mary, Blackbeard, Hornigold, Henry, the ship, and the treasure. She was the many-great-granddaughter of Blackbeard the Pirate, who had come from the dead to help them find his treasure, release his soul, and in the process forge a family out of women who had never met, yet had developed a family tradition that would end with her.

Emily was more resolute now than ever to keep the baby she carried.

She had walked back to the funeral home. Mark was still on duty; no time had passed yet she felt like she had been gone a lifetime. He appeared happy to see her again.

"Hi," Emily said, not sure how to start.

"Hi."

"I've been thinking."

"Yeah, so have I."

"I want to keep this baby. I know we don't know each other very well, but we can start at the beginning with a few dates and see where things go."

"That's pretty much what I was thinking too." Mark smiled. It was a nice smile.

Twelve years later, the girl sitting to her other side, fiddling with her hand-held video game, had her eyes and mouth, her father's nose, and coloring. It hadn't been easy, Emily reflected, but on the whole, it was the right decision and she and Mark made a good team.

Maggie walked up to the trio and smiled.

"It's time, the tea shop is there." Emily smiled at her mother, pleased that three generations of Teach women were together. Despite her death on the rocks in 1719, Maggie the real person had still been born, gotten pregnant by a dashing Frenchman, and given Emily up for adoption. And lived.

"Did you tell your Mom where you would be?" Maggie asked.

"Yes, although I'm not sure she'll even know we were gone. She did say she wanted to come; I wasn't sure if that would work. What do you think?"

Maggie considered this for a moment. "I don't know how the tea shop portal works but it's worth a try. You should bring her next time. Is Mark going along?"

"No, Mark is not going," he answered, rousing from his nap, "no way am I getting in the middle of the Teach women. I've heard enough about them to know I'm safer here."

"Grace," Emily straightened her child's hair, "do you remember the story I told you about the pirates, and the ship and the treasure?" Her hand went to the gold necklace she wore around her neck and the locket with the picture of her mother on one side and her daughter on the other. She had returned with a gold chain, two rings, a couple of gold bracelets, and a handful of rare coins. She had been able to sell these for over a million dollars. The locket and the ring would stay with her forever.

Her daughter heaved a put-upon sigh.

"Yes, Moooommmm." She drew out the Mom to emphasize her exasperation. "You wrote a book, remember?" She heaved another labored sigh and turned sideways on the bench to put her back to her mother and grandmother. Emily smiled at her daughter's back.

"Well, this is pretty much where it started," she said having learned to keep plowing ahead despite how little interest her daughter showed in the family story. The family story: she had written that line so many times in the past year she couldn't count. It turned out that the arts did run in her blood. The 'Family Story' had been the working title of the book she wrote documenting the unbelievable tale of finding Blackbeard's treasure.

The publisher eventually settled on "Blackbeard's Women," which she didn't like but settled on to get it published.

She felt the title put too much emphasis on the man Blackbeard when the real story of heroics and strength were the women, her forebears. The book resonated with women across the country, landing her on Oprah's reading list and on Good Morning America. The research she had done to write the story had drawn her closer than ever to the women she had met but had not come to know as well as she would have liked.

Emily remembered the day after returning that she told her mother she was pregnant and shared the story of *The Maryann*. Meeting her biological mother left Emily with two mothers. Maggie would never be the mother Sydney was and Sydney remained Mom. Maggie was Maggie.

Emily's stomach still tightened when she thought of that conversation. She had joined her mother on the couch one night for some television. In a commercial break, she took the remote and hit the mute button.

"Mom, can we talk?"

"Sure honey, what's up?"

"Please don't be mad at me."

Her mother looked at her with a *what have you done* look.

"It's sort of complicated, but starts with, I'm pregnant."

"What?!"

"It gets better, I traveled back in time, met my biological mother, grandmother, and others, found a treasure, and brought some back." She had pulled a gold ring from her pocket and handed it to her mother.

"That's quite a fairytale young lady, now let's start with the truth."

Emily knew it wasn't going to be easy to explain that this was the truth.

The treasure's secret remained a secret, although Emily had proof that each of her ancestors had found their way back to the little hour-glass shaped island, something she had not done yet.

One month after she had returned, she received a letter, sent to her adopted mother, from the adoption agency, saying they had located a letter from a lawyer in Atlanta, informing her about a safety deposit box in her name. In the box were more gold and jewels and a slip of paper with an address, which led her to Maggie.

Unsure at first of how it would play out, she introduced Maggie to her Mother and the three of them set off to learn as much as they could of the descendants of Blackbeard the pirate. Researching her genealogy had brought a level of peace to her as she started her own family. The joint effort to uncover Emily's history brought them closer together, and Emily's mothers had forged a friendship uniting the little family together. Her mother's shock at having her only daughter suddenly pregnant was tempered by the excitement of being a grandmother, and the truth of the story as they unraveled it, one woman at a time.

The bits of treasure that each of her ancestors had been able to bring back were evident in the stories and records they found. Emily and her two mothers spent the last twelve years exploring every one of the crewmembers and learning how each had taken the treasure and used it to better their circumstances. She read about Lieutenant Maynard and his crusade to eliminate all the pirates, which failed. Even to this very day, pirates sail the seas and skies, menacing shipping lanes and air travel. History wasn't clear on whether Hornigold had survived pirate hunts of the day, the legend of his life overshadowing the circumstances of his death.

Emily and Mark dated for five months before realizing they were in love and married before the baby was born. They chose to use the money gained from selling the treasure to buy a house. It was the responsible thing to do. They had not gone back to visit the island because it was part of a country with a brutal dictator. Someday in the future but by then the treasure would be gone. It was clear that each woman only hinted that the gold and jewels they were selling were pirate treasure. Emily had come to realize that the real treasure of Blackbeard was the family of women he had spawned and the life with Mark and Mary that Emily had gained.

"See you later," Mark said as Emily, Grace, and Maggie joined hands and walked into the little tea shop that looked like it had been pulled from the back of a long-forgotten shelf and fluffed out and crammed in between two trendy boutiques.

ABOUT THE AUTHOR

L.G.Reed (L.A.Reed) first published an award-winning short story in high school then went on to a career in advertising and engineering before settling on California's central coast and devoting herself to writing. You can follow her on Facebook at https://www.facebook.com/authorlindareed/ or her website: www.authorlindareed.com.

BOOKS BY L. G. REED

The Maiden Voyage of *The Maryann* – YA/Women's Fiction

Sydney Porter: Dog Girl – Middle-Grade Fantasy

The Science of Defying Gravity – Middle-Grade Fiction

THE SCIENCE OF DEFYING GRAVITY

Cassie dreams of going to Space Camp to pursue her goal of becoming the first movie director/astronaut. Three things stand in her way: annoying brothers, money, and she doesn't like science. Can math and science-averse kid win the science fair to earn the money to go?

www.ingramcontent.com/pod-product-compliance
Lightning Source LLC
Chambersburg PA
CBHW060918180626
46817CB00004B/1308